Massacre at Maple Bluff

When Cade Kellerman and his gang bungled their robbery of a train and killed more than twenty passengers, they could not have known that the husband of one of those killed was himself a former bandit, who would stick at nothing to revenge himself on those he blamed for the loss of his wife. Together with an idealistic law student, Ben Walters sets out to track down and bring to justice the Kellerman Gang; even if he should lose his own life in the attempt.

Massacre at Maple Bluff

Brent Larssen

A Black Horse Western

ROBERT HALE

ISBN 978-0-7198-2854-6

The Crowood Press
The Stable Block
Crowood Lane
Ramsbury
Marlborough
Wiltshire SN8 2HR

www.bhwesterns.com

Robert Hale is an imprint
of The Crowood Press

FLINTSHIRE SIR Y FFLINT	
C29 0000 0828 630	
Askews & Holts	18-Dec-2018
AF	£14.50
FLIHEAD	

CHAPTER 1

On a glorious summer's day in 1873, a group of a dozen or so men were working on the railroad tracks west of the town of Maple Bluff in Iowa. The appearance of these men suggested that digging the earth and levering up sleepers and rails in this way was not perhaps their usual occupation. They were not attired in the sort of rough clothes commonly donned by labourers of this kind. Indeed, from the look of them one would have said that they were in general, pretty sharp dressers. Another unusual circumstance was the amount of weaponry scattered around the site of their endeavours. In addition to the one or two pistols sported by every member of the band, there were carbines, scatterguns and hunting rifles leaning against packs or just lying on the ground. This was no wild part of the Indian territories, where sudden attack might readily be anticipated, but rather the placid and fertile farming country of the Midwest. The presence of so many guns indicated that trouble was in the wind.

Had an observer been able to hear, as well as see, the men working on the railroad that day, then matters would soon have been made as plain as day. Their conversation was entirely made up of plans to spend shares in the $100,000 of gold bullion that was heading their way on board the Chicago, Rock Island and Pacific Express. Rather than laying or repairing railroad tracks, these men were presently engaged upon sabotaging them, with the intention of derailing the express as it came around the bend and headed along the final straight run to Maple Bluff.

'I surely could do without labouring away in the sun like a damn' coolie,' observed one of the men toiling away at the railroad tracks, 'Might as well get me a job on the C & O road and be done with it.'

'Time was,' remarked the man wielding a mattock at his side, 'As a body only had to wave a red lantern in front of a locomotive and then help his self to what was needful.'

There were murmurs of assent to this latest speaker and muttered imprecations about the undesirability of slaving away like men on an old-time plantation in order to bring a railroad train to a halt and allow it to be plundered. The leader of the band cut short these complaints by growling in a menacing tone, 'Any o' you boys object to my plans or's minded to ride with another outfit, that man best collect his gear and ride on out, you hear what I tell you?

This announcement was received in sullen silence

and they looked watchfully at the man who had spoken. Not one of them was inclined to challenge his authority and the truth of the case was that he had led them so far to unparalleled success in their chosen career of bushwhacking and banditry. When Cade Kellerman had run his eyes over each man in turn and established that not one of them wished to stand up to him, he thought it generous to temper his authority with explanation. Kellerman said, 'Happen I don't need to remind you-all of what chanced down in Missouri, not three weeks since?'

This sobered the men up and no mistake. They all knew about what was known in some quarters as the 'Missouri Massacre'. A bunch of road agents had thought to expand their field of operations and tackle something a little more substantial than the stages that were their usual prey. On the night of June 20th, they had waylaid a train passing through a secluded spot. There was a full moon that night, which was unfortunate for the would-be robbers.

After swinging a red light as the train approached, causing it to slow down and then halt, in apprehension of danger ahead, the six men who aimed to relieve the passengers of their watches, jewellery and cash-money dismounted and drew nigh to the locomotive. Whereupon, all hell broke loose. The driver and guard commenced firing at the men, which prompted a number of private individuals who were travelling on the train to take similar action. It was a turkey shoot, with the bandits taken altogether

unawares. There had been just a few too many robberies of this kind since the end of the war and
people were getting sick and tired of the business.

Every man-Jack of the bandits died that night.
Their bodies were subjected to various indignities by
the angry passengers, before being loaded aboard
the luggage van. At the next town, the bloody corpses
were unceremoniously bundled out of the van and
then propped up against a wall of the depot. A paste-
board sign was placed nearby, with the message
painted on it in red: 'This is what happens to robbers
here'.

Kellerman could see that his words had worked to
some effect. Each man was remembering the killings
in Missouri and perhaps reflecting that there were
worse things in this world than swinging a pickaxe
under a hot sun. He said, 'I don't aim for us-all to be
making a regular custom o' digging the earth so. But
we're in sore need of funds right now and I don't see
as we have another choice.'

'How long we got 'fore that express comes?' asked
one of the men.

'Lacks but a half-hour, by my reckoning,' said
Kellerman, after consulting his pocket watch, 'The
chief advantage of our present scheme is that everybody on that train'll be so shook up by it crashing,
that they're like to be thinking more on how best to
save their own lives, rather than reaching for their
weapons. They won't know as it's a robbery, not 'til
we's aboard and facin' 'em down with our guns.'

So it was that the men known across three states as the 'Kellerman Gang' set to in earnest until they had levered up the rails from their bed and disconnected a section, twisting it to one side, so that it pointed not straight ahead, but rather to the sandy loam that lay nigh to the railroad line.

Mr Benjamin Walters was, by general estimation, one of the leading citizens of Maple Bluff. Since moving to the area almost twenty-five years earlier, he had built up the biggest spread for fifty miles in any direction. He employed many young men from the town and the money that was paid to them in wages was then spent in Maple Bluff; contributing to the prosperity of the storeowners and saloon keepers. It was generally reckoned that Walters' arrival in Maple Bluff had been a blessing and that his industry and enterprise had in large measure served to rejuvenate the town and attract further investment. In short, he was seen as no mean benefactor to Maple Bluff.

On that sunny, July afternoon, Benjamin Walters was lounging around at the railroad depot, waiting for his wife to return from visiting family back east. 'Lounging' would perhaps not be the best way to describe what Walters was doing while waiting for the train to arrive. Although he was strolling back and forth along the platform in an apparently aimless and absent-minded fashion, his thoughts were in reality racing along as fast as could be. He was preoccupied with a new scheme, which would allow he and his wife to take things a mite easier than they had been for the last few years. Both Walters and his wife Jenny were now around the sixty mark and while she had been away, the thought had taken root in Walters' mind that they deserved to let up a little now.

Apart from his business interests, Benjamin Walters was a Justice of the Peace and town councilman, in addition to serving as governor of the local school and being involved in various charitable enterprises. His wife's time was also fully committed to many worthy causes, to such an extent that they sometimes scarcely saw each other during the day. It was, Walters had decided in Jenny's absence, time for all this to change. As he mused on all this while awaiting her arrival that afternoon, he would have been vastly surprised to discover that his wife's thoughts were at that very moment running along precisely similar lines.

As the express thundered along, about to enter the final straight approach to Maple Bluff, Jennifer Walters was chatting amiably to a chance acquaintance whom she had happened to make, while sitting beside her on the journey from Jordan's Crossing. She said, 'It ain't that I don't enjoy all that I do, but I'd like for me and Ben to spend more time together and let other things go hang. I dare say that sounds right selfish!'

'Not a bit of it,' replied Harriet Carson, 'I do

declare you've the right notion. What is this life if you can't devote it to caring about your own self and your family? I reckon from all you've been a telling of me, you deserve it.'

'You truly think so?'

'That I do. Surely your orphans' asylum and school and all the rest of it would function well enough if you and your husband were to take off for a few months?'

'You don't know what a mercy it is to hear somebody tell me so. Soon as we reach Maple Bluff, I'm going to tell that husband of mine straight. Thank you so much.'

Digging up the rails had been arduous enough, but manhandling a section of them and ensuring that they were lined up away from the ones in front had taken a deal of sweating and cursing from the dozen men who were hoping to raid the secure van trailing along at the end of the express. By the time they had accomplished this end, the plume of smoke that signalled the coming of the locomotive could be seen in the distance and there was scarcely time for them to stow their gear away and lead their horses behind the rocks and out of sight from those looking from the windows as the Chicago, Rock Island and Pacific Express hove into view.

There had been no intention on the part of Cade Kellerman and his boys actually to cause harm to anybody during the robbery, but nor had there been any real attempt to avoid injury. They simply didn't care who might get hurt, so long as they got their hands on the gold being carried on the express. As it chanced, the whole venture very nearly passed off without bloodshed. Once the locomotive ran off the tracks and began ploughing through the loose soil, it looked at first as though it would simply continue in its path, gradually slowing down until the whole train came to a smooth halt. The trouble was that when a lump of steel weighing many tons is speeding along at forty-five miles an hour, the slightest little thing that interrupts its motion can have unforeseen consequences. So it was with the express. The first thirty or forty feet went smoothly enough and then, for reasons that nobody ever established, the locomotive bucked like a colt and tipped over onto its side.

Once the locomotive halted abruptly, the line of cars behind it then smashed one into the other; some of them also overturning. By the time that the whole train had shuddered to a halt, almost the only wagon still upright was the secure van at the very rear; which of course suited the bandits very well. Ignoring the cries of the injured, they mounted up and rode down on the wrecked train.

The man charged with guarding the contents of the van was not cast at all in the heroic mould. When once he realized that the derailing of the express was an act of hostility, rather than a tragic accident, he simply unlocked the door and walked out of the van with his hands above his head. It was in this character that Kellerman and the others encountered him as they reined in at the rear of the train. Kellerman said, 'You the guard?'

'Not any more!' replied the fellow frankly, which statement elicited a gale of laughter from the gang. Even Kellerman smiled as he asked about gaining access to the gold bullion.

'Gold bullion?' said the man, 'We ain't carrying no bullion.'

'The hell you talkin' about, boy?' said Cade Kellerman, 'You got a hundred thousand worth o' gold bars stashed away in that there van. Don't lie to me now.'

'I ain't lying to you,' the guard said, shrugging his shoulders, 'Go see for your own selves.'

'You're damned right we will!' said another member of the gang. He and a couple of others dismounted and clambered up to investigate the van. They emerged a few seconds later to declare angrily, 'He's right! There ain't nothin' in there beyond a few letters.'

Baffled and furious, Kellerman rounded on the guard, asking angrily, 'What's to do? Where's that gold as was supposed to be carried on this run?'

'It's no affair o' mine,' said the young man, just a mite too saucily for Cade Kellerman's taste. 'Whyn't you ask them as owns the railroad?'

Already feeling the loss of face consequent upon leading his gang on what had turned out to be a snipe hunt, Kellerman took this jaunty response very

ill. He said, 'No affair of yours, is it? You think so?'
Then he pulled the rifle from where it rested in its
scabbard at front of his saddle, worked around into
the breach and drew down on the man in front of
him. 'Still say it ain't your affair?' he enquired in a
soft, but deadly voice.

Even now, further bloodshed could have been
averted, had the young man had the sense that the
good Lord gave to a goat. This proved not to be the
case, for he said in that same cocksure tone, 'Killing
me won't magic up your gold!' Whereupon
Kellerman shot him. The ball took the fellow in the
belly and he stared down at the wound in surprise,
remarking stupidly, 'I wouldn't o' thought you'd o'
shot a man for that!'

'Shows how wrong you can be,' replied Cade
Kellerman and fired once more; this time straight
through the fellow's head; whereupon he proceeded
to drop down dead on the spot.

Benjamin Walters and one or two others were
becoming quite concerned by the time that a half
hour had passed since the express should have
pulled into the depot at Maple Bluff. Walters, as the
person of most consequence, took it upon himself to
investigate. He knocked on the door of the depot's
superintendent and asked, 'Any reason you know
why the express should be late in? Should have been
here knocking on five and thirty minutes since.'

'Well Mr Walters,' said the man apologetically, 'I

can't say as there is any reason as I know of. We received word from the telegraph that it left Jordan's Crossing on time and there's nothing in the way o' bridges or obstacles as I can think of that would account for the delay.'

It was to be another two hours, two hours of increasing anxiety among those waiting to meet relatives and friends who were expected in on the express, before a rider galloped into Maple Bluff and headed straight for the depot. He had a grim look on his face and some of those standing around hailed him immediately, asking if he was the bearer of tidings. He said, before even dismounting, 'I was riding along the track. Came to the wreck, must've been only a short while after it come off the tracks. Ridden hard ever since to bring word here.'

'Wreck?' said Benjamin Walters, 'You mean there's been an accident?'

'Accident? Hell, no!' said the rider, before collecting himself and noticing that there were ladies present. He continued, 'There was no accident. It was a robbery. They bungled it and the train was all smashed up.'

'Anybody hurt?' called a man from the crowd.

'Yes, a heap o' folks, some of 'em killed stone dead,' was the alarming answer.

No time was lost in gathering together provisions and medical supplies and putting together a rescue party to go out to the aid of the stricken railroad train. Walters was at the forefront of these preparations. He had come to the depot in the buggy, in order to fetch home his wife. Now, he begged the loan of a horse from the livery stable and led the expedition along the road to Jordan's Crossing, which ran parallel to the railroad tracks.

When they reached the scene of the tragedy, the group of riders reined in without a word to each other, so awful was the sight that they beheld. Some people were hobbling round with makeshift bandages around their heads, bandages that were soaked with blood. Others were sitting dazed, just staring into space, too shocked to react to what was going on around them. Then there was the line of bodies, laid in a row by the tracks. Some attempt had been made to cover these corpses decently, but they still presented a dreadful tableau. There were at least twenty of them.

Benjamin Walters got down from his horse and walked slowly over to the bodies. He somehow knew already what he would find and so it proved; for he recognized at once the maroon dress worn by one of the lifeless forms. Even though somebody had covered the face with a shawl, he knew that it was his beloved Jenny. Without a word, he walked over and lifted the cloth from the upper part of his wife's body and stared into her dead face. He didn't howl with anguish or burst into a fit of weeping, because that was not his way. Instead, he strolled over to where one of the liveried attendants from the express was talking about the robbery to some of the men who'd just arrived from Maple Bluff. He said to the man in a low voice, 'Who did this?'

'Well sir,' began the man in a fussy and self-important way, 'I couldn't take oath in a court of law, but. . . .'

Walters had neither time nor inclination to listen to pointless talk, so he cut in and said quietly, 'Just you tell me now what you suspect. Who did this thing?'

'I saw a poster not two days ago, and the man who took us down today was either that very man or his twin brother. Name of Kellerman.'

'Cade Kellerman would that be?'

'That's the name, for a bet. Why I guess that. . . .' But the man was speaking to thin air. Walters had strode off as soon as he had the name he wanted. He went up to one of the men with whom he had rode from town and took him to one side. He said, 'Bob, I don't see that I can be a lot of use here. I'm going back to Maple Bluff now and I'll tell what they need to send out here. You'll be wanting a cart or two for them bodies.'

The other man looked searchingly at Walters and asked, 'Was Mrs Walters. . . .'

'She was. Might I ask that you take care to see that she is laid gentle and brought back to town?'

Bob Brewster stretched out his hand and said, 'You got my word on it, Ben.' The two of them clasped hands briefly and then Walters mounted up and headed back towards Maple Bluff.

Once he had set things in motion in town and fended off the sympathy of his fellow citizens, Benjamin Walters returned to his ranch. Briefly, he apprised the two live-in servants of what had occurred and, after acknowledging their commiserations, Walters went up to the attic. Dusk was falling and so he took with him a lamp. There, in a stout chest, secured by a strong padlock, were some pieces of equipment that he felt that he would be needing over the next few weeks.

The chest had not been opened in over twenty years and the lock was accordingly rusty and stiff, but it eventually yielded. Inside the box were various mementoes of Benjamin Walters' old life; the one that he had put off after moving to Maple Bluff and meeting Jenny. Beneath some bolts of mouldering cloth was a bundle of old newspapers, the most recent of which was dated February 1850. Walters lifted these out, to reveal a bundle wrapped in oiled cloth.

It was absurd, but he was almost fearful to touch the things after all these years. But there, that was a lot of foolishness. He shook his head impatiently and took out the bundle, which he set on the floor in front of him. He moved the lamp closer and then undid the string holding the cloth in place. On undoing the knots, Walters took out from the parcel a holster and belt, made of black leather. He laid this to one side and then lifted the copper powder-flask out as well. Despite knowing that his almost superstitious dread was ridiculous, he stayed crouching by the chest for a few seconds, just looking at the gun-belt and flask. Then he stretched out his hand and picked up the pistol. It was a .44 calibre Colt Walker and when he had hidden it away in that chest, this six-shot pistol was the most modern and up-to-date handgun one could hope to possess. Now, it was next door to being an antique, so rapidly had things changed during and after the War Between the States. Still and all, Walters reckoned that the piece would serve his purpose well enough; which was to track down and kill with his own hands every man who had been involved in wrecking that train and killing his wife. The Walker was an absolute monster; fifteen inches long and weighing in at over four and a half pounds. It was meant really as a cavalry sidearm, something to be kept in a holster at the side of a saddle, rather than hanging from a man's belt. Still, this weapon had served Walters well enough and would surely do the trick now. He stood up and tucked the pistol in his belt.

CHAPTER 2

All Abernathy Jackson has ever wanted was to be a
Pinkertons man. As a boy, he had read dime novels
in which heroic men from the Pinkertons detective
agency foiled train robberies or prevented assassina-
tions and, now that he was nineteen, he felt that the
time was ripe to fulfil his ambitions. In that year of
grace 1873, the Pinkerton National Detective Agency
had more men under arms than the entire federal
army. It was practically a parallel police force and
secret service. Indeed, for some years, the line
between Alan Pinkerton's organization and the official police and intelligence agencies was more than a
little blurred. This had been quite deliberate on
Pinkerton's part. Any man who sets up a private
company called the North-Western Police Agency
must surely know that some folk will get it muddled
up with the regular law. A few years down the line
and the Pinkertons set-up would have its wings

clipped, but for now it was riding high; very high indeed.

Because it was so famous and associated with any number of daring and successful operations, there was never any shortage of adventurous young fellows applying to join up with the Pinkertons agency. Those possessed of nothing more than great skill with deadly weapons were likely to be rejected. There were already plenty of strong-arm types in their employ. What they were chiefly looking for now were men with initiative and brains. True, they had to be able to handle themselves in a rough-house and not be afraid to shoot a man when the chips were down, but that wasn't the whole of it; not by a long chalk. Alan Pinkerton wanted something more. His staff were under instructions to pass on to their boss any letters or applications for jobs with the agency that stood out and indicated that the writer might have that something extra for which they were looking.

It was in this way that Abernathy Jackson had come to the attention of the great man, who had told his staff to arrange an interview with the boy. A whole heap of roughnecks and ne'er-do-wells were forever trying to obtain employment with Pinkertons, but it was a rare event indeed for a young man in his first year of studying law at Harvard to offer to abandon his studies and sign up with the Pinkerton National Detective Agency. The boy was from a good family too, if Alan Pinkerton was any judge of such things. Which was why on that afternoon of Thursday, July

23rd 1873, Pinkerton was sitting in his Chicago office, waiting for Abernathy Jackson to be ushered into his presence.

'Sit ye doon, sit ye doon young fella!' exclaimed Pinkerton cordially, when the eager and nervous youth had been shown in. It was a quarter of a century since Alan Pinkerton had left his native land, but those twenty-five years had done nothing to soften his Scottish brogue. Even his closest subordinates found it hard at times to understand what their boss was saying. 'Noo, laddie,' he continued, 'Ye've had yoursel' an eddication, which is more'n I did. Ah left school at ten, d'ye know that?'

'No sir, I did not.'

'Aye well, it's the truth for all that. Tell me noo, what would ye say intelligence is?'

'Sir?' asked Abernathy Jackson, bewildered by the course that the interview was taking.

'Intelligence,' said Pinkerton, 'What d'ye think ah mean by it?'

'Well sir, I can think of two entirely separate and distinct meanings,' said Jackson, puzzled but glad that the conversation seemed to be tending towards semantics; a pet interest of his. 'Firstly, it can mean the ability to make use of knowledge and information. We call a man intelligent if he has that ability. Then again, it can be used to mean the collection of information of military or political value.'

Alan Pinkerton gazed at the young man with unfeigned admiration and said, 'Och, what a thing it is to be educated. Why, it's as good as a play to listen to you talk, sonny. Well noo, I make nae doot that ye've the first of those two meanings. I'm sure ye have a fund of intelligence. What aboot the second thing? How d'ye rank there?

'I'm not sure I understand you sir.'

'I've thousands o' men on m'pay roll as can shoot. I want people to find things out for me. I see you're at Harvard, so you're sharp enough. You go off now and bring me back some information about villainy, something none of my men know about. Do that an' I'll gie ye a job. Bring me intelligence about robbers, bushwhackers, road agents, what have ye.'

When Benjamin Walters had fetched up in Maple Bluff in the fall of 1850 with enough money to buy three hundred acres of good pasture, nobody in the town knew anything at all about him. Once settled, he had set about buying more land, until he was the biggest landowner in Baldwin County. Where his money had come from before he began farming, nobody knew. The fact was that Ben Walters had been a fine soldier, who fought valiantly in the Mexican War, leaving the army when the war ended in 1848. He had been all but penniless when he became a civilian once more and so determined to spend two years acquiring as much money as he could by any means needful. The easiest and quickest way of getting together the cash necessary to start a decent-sized farm seemed to Walters at that time to be robbery.

At the age of thirty-five and with the better part of twenty years' soldiering behind him, few men were better fitted than Benjamin Walters to prey on stage coaches and knock over banks. He operated chiefly in Texas, slipping south across the border into Mexico as and when the going grew a little too hot for him. It took Walters a little under the two years for which he had budgeted to get together the money he needed to purchase a good spread of pasture-land. It was a matter of some pride to him that he had hurt nobody during his brief career as a bandit. He'd certainly killed plenty and enough men during the Mexican War and also when fighting Indians in the west, but never once had he had cause to shoot anybody when carrying out a robbery.

Soon after settling in Maple Bluff, he had met Jennifer, who was the daughter of a pastor. He began courting her in the winter of 1850 and they were wed the following spring. She was just twenty years of age and her father was a mite uneasy about her marrying a man approaching forty. Howsoever, it all worked out for the best and they had twenty-two years of blissfully happy life together. Their three children ranged in age from nineteen to twenty-one and were all living lives of their own by the time that their mother was slain in the bungled raid on the express.

On the evening of Jennifer Walters' funeral, the mourners had all departed. One of Benjamin's sons was in Europe, but twenty-two-year-old Miriam and her younger brother Joshua were both staying at

24

their childhood home for a few nights. At nine that evening, they sat at the kitchen table as their father reasoned out his plans to them. He said, 'Josh, I want that you should stop here for a month or so, if you will. Keep the place running. Can you do that for me? '

'Sure, Pa. I reckon I can take a break from college for a few weeks.'

'From all that I am able to collect,' said his father wryly, 'Your studies won't suffer. You ain't overburdened with book learning. Wonder it's worthwhile your staying there.'

'You going away for a spell?' asked Miriam. 'You want to come and stay with me, over in Jordan's Crossing?'

'No, I'm thankful for the offer, but I reckon not.'

'Where you going?' asked his son.

Benjamin Walters looked at his son in surprise and said, 'Why, I'm going to hunt down those sons of bitches who took your mother's life. You didn't think as I'd let them get away with this, did you?'

Abernathy Jackson left the headquarters of the Pinkerton Detective Agency in a state of high excitement. The famous Alan Pinkerton had actually spoken to him and said that he was the kind of man that he wanted! Why, he was already next door to being a Pinkertons man. It wanted only a little application on his part and his future there would be assured. Where to start though, that was the question.

It was almost midday and so Jackson thought he'd find an eating house and think matters over.

After ordering a bowl of broth, Jackson sat down at a table and was pleased to find that there was a newspaper lying on the table, so that customers might catch up on the news while they ate. It was a copy of that day's *Chicago Daily Tribune* and as soon as his eyes fell upon the main story, Abernathy Jackson knew what he would need to do to gain employment with Pinkertons. The headline declared: LATEST SANGUINARY OUTRAGE OF THE KELLERMAN GANG. The article below gave details of the wrecking of the express train on which Benjamin Walters' wife had been travelling. It appeared that no fewer than twenty-eight people had lost their lives in the course of the attempted robbery. Here was a prize to take to Mr Pinkerton! Even away over east at Harvard, Jackson had heard of the depredations of Cade Kellerman and his gang of cut-throats. Only think, if he could be the one to supply the information leading to the capture of these desperados! It was the very thing. After supping his broth, the young man snatched up his hat and headed out of the eatery. He didn't have much idea how to proceed, but he had the optimism of youth, combined with limitless energy and enthusiasm. He just knew that he'd be able to get a line on those men. The only shooting that Abernathy Jackson had ever undertaken had been hunting squirrels as a schoolboy, but he supposed that in an enterprise of this kind, that he would need a weapon of some sort and so determined to find the necessary kind of store without delay.

It was plain as a pikestaff to Cade Kellerman that the men who rode with him were not best pleased about the way things had turned out. The reckoning they'd been given was that each one of them stood to gain somewhat in the region of ten thousand dollars for the afternoon's work. Not only had they none of them made a cent from the enterprise, they were being hunted now not only by the regular law, but also by Pinkerton's boys. The railroad had put a price on their head; five thousand for Kellerman himself, dead or alive, and two thousand a piece for the rest of them. There was to be no question of anybody being afforded the opportunity to turn state's evidence; all those who'd had a part in the massacre were like to hang if taken.

Men from the Pinkerton agency were now riding shotgun on most of the trains running through Iowa; so that game was out, but it was clear enough that the Chicago, Rock Island and Pacific Railroad Company was not stopping there. It was paying men to track down those responsible for the death of twenty-eight of its passengers.

In a clearing in a pine forest just north of Cedar Rapids, Cade Kellerman and his boys were seated around a fire, on which a pot of coffee was warming. They didn't live out in the wild like this all the time, like wolves and bears, but all had homes to go to when they were not out on the scout. Only thing was, there was no desire to lead either the law or Pinkertons to their families; there being no telling if even now they might not be being trailed. It seemed to them to make more sense to wait a space for memory of what was becoming known generally as the Maple Bluff Outrage to fade a little. None of them had much in the way of cash money and it would have been just sitting up and begging for trouble to ride into a town right then; so the eleven men were compelled to hunt for what vittles they could in the open country and hope that things might quieten down after a spell. They had brought down a buck that day and roasted it over the open fire, in the ashes of which they were now brewing coffee.

'I could surely do with side vegetables for this here,' remarked one man. 'Or even bread wouldn't come amiss.'

Kellerman, whose mood was no sweeter than anybody else's, growled, 'Happen you want to book into a hotel in Cedar Rapids? I hear where the Metropole does a fine dinner.'

'There's no call for to mock him,' replied Jack Harker. This man had it in mind to wrest control of the gang from Cade Kellerman and had not missed any opportunity since the abortive robbery of the express to undermine Kellerman's authority, which to tell the truth was a little shaky anyway by now.

Harker continued, 'Seems to me as some plain speaking's in order. Which is as much to say, how we come to this pass and what's to be done 'bout it.'

There was a silence after Harker spoke and the others eyed their boss warily, wondering what might chance next. They had all of them had ample proofs of Cade Kellerman's vicious temper and short way with dissenters over the last twelve months and nobody was overly keen to be the one upon whose head the lightning might descend. They were all of them ticked off at the turn of events, but only Jack Harker was bold enough to state the case openly.

'Speak plain, then,' said Kellerman, 'And tell us what's on your mind. Don't hold back none.'

'We done right good together,' began Harker, 'And I'll be the first to own it, but of late, things ain't precisely gone as smooth as could be wished.'

'No?' said Cade Kellerman amiably, 'You think not?'

'I know not and so do the rest of these boys. You screwed up over that train, Cade, and it ain't the first time neither.'

While Harker was speaking, Kellerman got to his feet and stretched, like he might have been getting the cramp from sitting in one spot for too long. He wriggled his ankles a little, which reinforced this impression. Then, like somebody just exercising his legs, he began walking around the clearing. He said to Jack Harker, 'Don't be being shy now, just tell

29

what's on your mind. We can reason the matter out together.'

Encouraged by these words into thinking that Cade Kellerman was backing down, Harker carried on, saying, 'To put it blunt, we's all stuck out here in the wild, with no money and none of us minded to go back to our homes, less'n we draw trouble to our own doorsteps. It happen before, now it happen again.'

Still acting casual and friendly, Kellerman strolled over to a tree and began picking aimlessly at the bark. Harker began to think that he really was in with a chance of seizing control and turning this from the 'Kellerman Gang' into something else again; perhaps the 'Harker Outfit' or something like that. So engrossed was he in these pleasant speculations, that Jack Harker didn't mark Kellerman leave off scratching at some tree and walk round instead, until he was behind Harker. Then before any of those sitting round the fire in that glade had any idea what might be about to happen, Cade Kellerman launched himself at Harker's back and knocked the man into the fire.

Harker squealed in pain as he found his cheek lying in the hot embers and began to rise. Kellerman though was on his back in an instant and, grasping both the other man's wrists, twisted them swiftly back; meaning that Harker was quite unable to lever himself up. His legs thrashed helplessly as the red-hot ashes singed his moustache and burned his face.

He shrieked in agony, 'Turn me loose, turn me loose! I'm being burned up here.'

'Being burned up are you?' said Kellerman harshly, 'By God, I've more'n half a mind to fry your brains out.' Neither Jack Harker nor any of the other men in the clearing had the mistaken impression that Kellerman was speaking metaphorically or uttering a baseless threat. If he said that he was planning to fry a man's brains, then the chances are that this was just precisely what he would do. Nobody loved Harker enough to intervene. The others simply watched and waited to see what would happen to their comrade.

There was, it was true, a spirit of discontent abroad, but the men in his gang looked to Kellerman to right things. He had led them to fortune before and no doubt he would do so in the future. Of one thing they were all sure; Cade Kellerman was the hard one. He was more fearless and daring than any of them and there was not one of them would have stood against him. As they watched Jack Harker's hair smouldering and wondered if Kellerman would indeed kill him, each of them was secretly glad that it was not he who was the object of their leader's wrath.

After waiting a few more seconds, Kellerman said to the helpless man upon whose back he was kneeling and whose wrists he held in a grip like iron manacles, 'If I consent to let you live, which by the by I ain't yet made up my mind to, you goin' to cause me grief in the future?'

'Mother o' God, let me up!'

'Answer my question first.'

'Swear to God, I won't ever trouble you. Please, please. . . .'

Satisfied that all the rest had now heard Harker begging piteously to be released and almost whimpering like a little girl, Kellerman stood up and said, 'You speak so to me another time and I'll kill you, you hear what I say? And the rest o' you too, listen to what I'm telling you. Our last scheme miscarried and that's the fact of it. But that don't signify, for I've an idea how we can get out o' this hole we're in, so listen up now.'

Time was when Benjamin Walters was able to vault onto a horse by running at his mount and then leaping up, hooking his left foot into the stirrup and so swinging himself into the saddle; all without the use of his hands. Those days were long gone and now, at sixty years of age, it was all that he could do to get on without use of a mounting-block. In recent years, Walters had been more accustomed to riding in a buggy than he was going horseback. After tacking up the mare, he decided to have one last coffee before riding out. He'd put a blanket roll at back of the saddle and some food to tide him over for a day or two. Although he knew some might think it foolish, he was determined to carry the same pistol on this expedition that he had all those years ago, before he settled down and became respectable. He accordingly had the heavy Walker hanging at his hip as well.

To his surprise, both his son and daughter were up and waiting for him in the kitchen. Walters grunted, 'It's not yet six. You're both early risers and no mistake.'

'Couldn't let you ride away like this, Pa,' said his son, 'I'm minded to come along with you.'

'You? It's mighty nice of you, but I'd feel easier in my mind to know you were here, tending to this place. But I'm thankful for the offer.' Benjamin Walters did not feel it necessary to add that he thought his son as soft as butter and no more use than a woman on an undertaking of this kind. He had observed with disapproval that Joshua had been openly weeping as his mother was laid to rest. In Walters' eyes, this was not how men behaved. He was himself broken up with grief, but he would do his grieving in private, just as soon as he had dealt with this little job of work.

Miriam said, 'I needs must say it, since nobody else will. You're too old for such a game. It'll be the death of you. Come and stay with me and leave this to the law.'

Benjamin Walters looked into his daughter's eyes and said softly, in a voice that caused her to shiver suddenly, as though a goose had walked over her grave, 'In this matter, I *am* the law.'

CHAPTER 3

It was all well and good to talk of finding out about the famous Kellerman Gang and bringing the information back to lay at Alan Pinkerton's feet, but the plain truth of the matter was that Abernathy Jackson had not the least idea how to begin such a quest. Buying a gun had been easy enough, although under what circumstances he might have to use it were far from clear to Jackson. He just felt that it was the kind of item that a Pinkerton's man should at least possess.

Studying the newspapers had indicated that Kellerman and his boys were popularly supposed to be hiding out somewhere a long way from the scene of their attack on the Chicago, Rock Island and Pacific Express. After giving the matter a good deal of thought and closely examining a map of the state of Iowa, Jackson purchased a railroad ticket. He had not so far vouchsafed to his mother and father anything on the subject of his attempt to fulfil his childhood ambition. So far as they knew, their son was spending part of the summer vacation from college with a friend and fellow student who lived in Massachusetts. In time, they would probably discover this deception, but by then it was Abernathy Jackson's fervent hope that he would have been positively engaged by the Pinkerton National Detective Agency.

Once he had settled into his seat on the train heading west to Cedar Rapids, Jackson took out a map and examined it carefully. He had an idea that if he only applied his mind to it, he should be able to second-guess a bunch of bandits. The excitement of the thing made him shiver with pleasure. He might have been nineteen years of age, but there were times, and this was one of them, when Abernathy Jackson was more like a schoolboy than a Harvard law student. Childlike at times he might have been, but Jackson was no fool. It had not taken much expenditure of brain-power for him to figure out that Kellerman and his gang would not have lingered for long in the vicinity of Maple Bluff. Feeling was running high against them in that part of Iowa and they would most likely be hanged out of hand or shot down like mad dogs should a posse catch up with them thereabouts. For this reason, Jackson had carried out a few calculations relating to the speed at which a horse could travel in twenty-four hours. He had then a rough figure for how far the bandits might currently be from Maple Bluff. After drawing a circle with a radius of this number of miles, centred on Maple Bluff, Abernathy Jackson had done some hard thinking and as a consequence had booked a railroad ticket to Cedar Rapids, county seat of Linn County in Iowa.

Jackson opened the map and examined the pencilled circle that he had drawn. He muttered to himself, 'Where does the wise man hide a leaf? Why, in a forest of course!' A man across the aisle gave him a strange look and so Jackson studied the map all the harder and pretended that he hadn't spoken. As long as that party of a dozen armed and desperate men were riding together through sparsely inhabited country, they would be pretty noticeable. If they rode into some little town, the case would not be much improved for them. As Abernathy Jackson had figured out the matter to himself the night before setting out on this journey, the wanted men's only hope of safety lay in losing themselves among a whole heap of people, in a big town or even a city. Well then, it was only a question of working out how far they could have travelled in the time available and then seeing what the nearest city would be that they could enter and blend in with the ordinary folk there. There was, according to the map, only one candidate for the role and it was Cedar Rapids. He might be on a snipe hunt, but Jackson didn't think it for a moment. He truly believed that within a few days, he might be the one to run to earth the notorious gang of robbers and maybe even find a way to hand them over to the law. What would Alan Pinkerton say to that?

Even as Abernathy Jackson settled into his seat for what promised to be a most thrilling adventure, another man was trotting his mount along a ridge of high land running south of the town of Independence. Benjamin Walters was in a sober frame of mind that morning, because the evening before, he had shot a man dead; the first time he had done such a thing since the end of the Mexican war in 1848. This is what happened.

The first couple of nights that Walters had spent out in the open had been hard. He was no longer a young man by anybody's reckoning and it had been almost a quarter century since he had slept anywhere other than in a bed. The first night had been torture, because his shoulders and hips seemed constantly to be assailed by sharp stones and uncomfortable twigs. He was that stiff the next morning that it was all that he could do to mount his horse. Still and all, it was worth it. If nothing else, this expedition was serving to take Walters' mind off the dreadful bereavement that he had suffered. The fact that he hadn't been weeping and wailing at the funeral didn't mean that he wasn't bowed down with grief; it only signified that he had set aside his grieving for a more convenient season. For now, the quest for vengeance upon which he had embarked was keeping his mind from dwelling on how broken up inside he was at the loss of his beloved wife.

The second night was a little easier and it seemed to Benjamin Walters that he had just got soft over the years, nothing more. It was a mercy that he was making this journey in high summer though and that there was no frost or snow to contend with. He got up on that second morning, feeling a little more sprightly and thinking that he should have taken a trip or two like this years ago to keep himself in shape. It was after spending that day riding briskly in the direction of Cedar Rapids that trouble struck.

The depression that afflicted the United States in those days was so severe and long-lasting that some men gave up all hope of their prospects improving or even of being able to gain any useful employment. They turned instead to various criminal activities to get by. A small number became famous bandits like Kellerman and his gang, but for many it was simply a question of robbing lone travellers; like the old-time highwaymen of England. As the sun was sinking towards the western horizon and Benjamin Walters was getting ready to halt for the night, a young man darted out in front of his horse and shouted, 'Stand to, or 'fore God I'll shoot you down!'

Walters had been riding along a narrow defile; with steep, scree-covered slopes rising high on either side. A few scrubby pines clung to the floor of this miniature valley and it was from behind one of these that the youthful robber had appeared.

This was not the first time in his life that Walters

had been accosted in this way, but never before by a youngster like this. The fellow brandishing a pistol at him was little more than a boy; he could scarcely be above seventeen or eighteen years of age at most. Walters said in a fatherly and reassuring tone, 'Steady on there, son. Mind what you're about with that weapon of yours.'

These friendly and well-meant words of advice seemed to infuriate the boy, because his face distorted in anger and he said in a low, ugly voice, 'I ain't your son, nor nothin' like it. Jest get down from that horse, or I'll kill you.'

'There's no call for such a thing,' said Walters quietly, 'See here now, I'm dismounting.'

A great sadness was upon him, for he knew that this was one of those dreadful situations where only one person would soon be left alive. He had not the slightest apprehension that this would not be him, but felt sorry that the one who was about to come off worst was almost a child. Once he was down from the mare, Walters said, 'Well then, what would you have me do next?'

'You can reach out that gun o' your'n from the holster. Easy though. Clench your fist and just stick y'finger through the trigger guard and hoist it out so. Then hand it me.'

With great reluctance, Benjamin Walters did as he had been bid. He lifted the heavy pistol from the artillery holster with his index finger, as instructed and then offered it, hilt first, to the boy, who reached out his hand eagerly. It was plain from the look on his face that this affair was going better than he had hoped. That was before Walters gave a flick of his wrist, which brought the barrel up, lifting the hilt of the pistol snugly into his hand, which he had at the same moment unclenched to receive it. Before the young man even realized what had just happened, Walters cocked the piece with his thumb and fired straight at the boy's chest. He followed this by kicking up sharply at the boy's gun, which was still pointing vaguely and menacingly in his direction; knocking it into the air.

The youngster looked thoroughly perplexed by the rapid turnabout in fortunes; he was now standing there empty-handed, while his putative victim covered him with a drawn pistol. He said, 'I didn't think I'd get shot!'

'That's the way of it, son,' said Walters. 'You never know who's like to be in that position at the end of the game.' The boy swayed on his feet and looked down wonderingly at the little hole in the front of his shirt. Then his legs began to give way and Walters holstered his piece and moved swiftly; so that he could place his arm round the young fellow's shoulders and help lower him gently to the ground.

The boy said, 'Am I hurt bad? I feel cold.'

There seemed little reason to frighten him by revealing that he probably had only a minute or two of life left in him and so Benjamin Walters said cheerfully, 'Ah, you'll do well enough. Looks to me like a flesh wound. How old are you?'

'I'll be sixteen this November coming.'

At the realization that he had gunned down a boy aged just fifteen, Walters felt sorrowful. There was nothing to be done to remedy the case though, for he could see the brilliant crimson colour of the blood from the chest wound; that vivid, bright hue that indicated a lung wound. Perhaps the youth could see in the older man's eyes the truth about his present condition, for he said in a weaker voice, 'I'm a dyin', ain't I?'

There seemed no point in further pretence and Walters said sombrely, 'That you are. You want a prayer or aught like that?'

The boy said, 'No, I reckon not.'

'Anything else I can do for you?'

But the youngster's eyes had closed, as though he was taking a little rest, and as Walters watched, he took one last shuddering breath and then let it out and did not breathe again.

Killing a man is a fearful business, even in time of war, and to kill somebody of such a tender age was even worse. Still, there'd been little choice in the matter and, regretful though he was, Benjamin Walters had not been about to allow anybody to interfere with his quest. He had no spade and so could not have buried the boy, even had he been minded to do so. He therefore contented himself with laying the corpse out on its back, with the hands folded across the breast. He removed his hat and stood by the body with his head bowed for a few moments and then mounted up and rode off towards Cedar Rapids. He'd been almost on the point of stopping for the night when he had been accosted, but he didn't somehow feel like camping in the vicinity of a corpse.

As Cade Kellerman had told the men with whom he rode, they were in grave danger of having their necks stretched if they didn't change track, and that right fast. He had said, half an hour after putting an end to Jack Harker's bid to topple him from his position of leader of the gang, 'Last few days, we been leaving a trail a child o' four could follow. Don't change our ways, it's a matter of time 'fore somebody catches up with us. We got regular law with most like a posse, we got the private boys from the railroad and we got Pinkertons men too, most like. I heard where Pinkerton's got some Indian trackers, those fellows'd find us if we went to China!'

'What d'you say as we should do?' asked somebody.

'The dozen of us riding through empty places like this,' replied Kellerman, 'We plough a furrow a yard deep. Anybody can see which way we went. We enter a little town, the self-same thing, everybody's going to remark upon us. We need to lose ourselves for a space, 'til things die down somewhat.'

'What you got in mind?' said another man.

'To set it out plain, we split up and ride into Cedar Rapids. There's enough folk there, that nobody'll notice another few who slip in one by one. The trail'll go stone cold and that'll be that. Sides which, I heard something lately 'bout the place, something as made me perk up my ears a mite. It might be that it'll make up for the reverse we lately suffered up by Maple Bluff.'

Being blessed with well-to-do parents who furnished him with a liberal allowance gave Abernathy Jackson a distinct advantage when it came to travelling round and waiting for something to happen. He was able to draw on his money by telegraphic transfer from a city like Cedar Rapids and his mother and father were content to let their favoured son occupy his time as he saw fit during the summer vacation from college. True, they would have had a blue fit had they known what he was about right now, but mercifully they had not the least notion of what he was up to. That he was hoping to abandon his study of law in order to become a private police officer would have horrified his mother beyond all measure. Still, there it was. This was his life and he had to live it as he saw fit.

Cedar Rapids was a lively and flourishing city and it struck the young man that had he not been there on business, so to speak, then this would be a good place to have a little fun. He marked it down mentally as somewhere to visit for pleasure at a later date. For now though, his sole, immediate and direct aim was to set a watch for the Kellerman Gang and see if he could find a way of handing them over on a plate to Mr Pinkerton. That would surely be a worthy prize and guarantee him a place in the agency. Since arriving in town, Jackson had heard something that suggested that he might be on the right track and that not only was Cedar Rapids the logical destination for Cade Kellerman and his boys if they were hoping to evade justice, but that there might be another and eminently practical reason for them to find their steps directed to the city.

Most people have heard of 'gold rushes', when a host of hopeful prospectors, desirous of making their fortune, descend upon a district where gold has been discovered. California's 1849 gold rush was a prime example of the phenomenon. Fewer folk though know anything of 'silver rushes'. This is because silver is more difficult to extract from ores and is less apt to be found in its natural form, but is chiefly bound up with other metals, such as lead. This means that extracting silver from the surrounding rocks, howsoever abundantly it may be present, is a more taxing business than simply panning for gold and coming up with nuggets of the pure article.

When huge reefs of silver had come to light in Nevada a few years previously, mining on an industrial scale had soon commenced. The government in Washington had soon concerned itself in the matter, seeing in the vast quantities of precious metal an opportunity to mint coins where the raw materials were present, rather than digging it out in one place, refining it elsewhere and then transporting the metal to a mint at a third location. So it was that a federal mint was established in Carson City, with all the silver required for the enterprise being right at hand.

What Abernathy Jackson had overheard while eating at the hotel into which he had booked, was that Cedar Rapids was the main distribution centre for the silver dollars minted in Carson City. There didn't seem to be any particular secret about this; the two men whom he overheard were joking about the amount of bullion that the First National Bank of Iowa must have in its vaults now, after the arrival of the latest train from Nevada. From what he could gather, the new coins were sent south from Cedar Rapids to Indiana, Kansas and Oklahoma, as well as east to Chicago.

After gathering this intelligence, Jackson was so excited that he simply could not remain seated; he needed to stride about a little and digest both his food and the news that he had acquired. The one was easy enough; young men's stomachs being famously able to absorb pretty much anything in the way of nutrition without any great effort. Absorbing and weighing the significance of what he had heard that tended to large amounts of precious metal in the vault of the city's main bank was something else again. It had been one thing to work out as a theoretical exercise just where the Kellerman gang might be headed. Finding that he had probably been right and that if so then he would soon be coming up against some of the most murderous

45

rogues currently loose in the United States was another thing. The amiable young man began to wonder if he had perhaps taken a wrong turn somewhere and if he wouldn't be best advised to book a railroad ticket back to Boston as soon as he could do so.

Being a Justice of the Peace, even a couple of days ride from his own town proved to be very useful for Ben Walters. One of the little towns en route to Cedar Rapids was Redwood and he decided to break his journey here for a night; mainly so that he could get washed and shaved and spare his aching body by sleeping a night in a proper bed. He had a slight acquaintance with the sheriff here and hoped to pump him for a little information germane to his self-appointed task. After booking a room above the Crooked Arrow saloon and getting a shave, Walters called on Sheriff Charles Grant in his office on Main Street.

'Why, what brings you to these parts, Mr Walters?' asked Sheriff Grant, when Walters walked into his little office, 'You here in an official capacity? Come with a warrant or suchlike? Pull up a chair and we'll see what can be done.'

The two men got along whenever their paths crossed and so Grant felt that he could josh a little with the other. When Walters had sat down and apprised him of recent events, the sheriff looked horrified and regretted his earlier jovial greeting. He had, of course, heard of the raid on the railroad, but had no idea that Ben Walters' wife had been numbered among the casualties. He said, 'I'm mighty sorry for your loss. Whenever I met Mrs Walters, she was always very kind to me. I'm not clear though what you hope to achieve now.'

'Well, you could say that while I'm passing through, I wouldn't mind a little legal advice.'

'Well, you're the law up in Maple Bluff. I would've thought you know as much law as me, most likely more. If you want civil law, you could step down the street a pace and consult old Jacob Wexford, the attorney. I'll wager he knows more law than a small-town sheriff like me.'

'Yes,' said Ben Walters slowly, 'If I was minded to buy a house or enter into a contract, then I make no doubt that an attorney could help. He might not be as well versed in the sort of law I'm asking about. I don't know the answer, but you might.'

'Go on. What's to do?'

'It's about citizen's arrests. If I find a wanted man, I can take him in charge and bring him to the nearest peace officer or court of law, that's correct isn't it?'

Sheriff Grant rubbed his chin meditatively. 'As far as it goes, that's true, yes. I hope this isn't tending where I suspect it is, though.'

'And if the man won't go, I can use deadly force in an extreme case, is my understanding.'

'Whoa, this is just as I feared. You're minded to

47

reckon with those as killed your wife. It won't do. You can't take the law into your hands like that.'

Benjamin Walters face hardened and he said softly, 'Nobody can tell me what I can and can't do. Is it true that I can use deadly force to make a citizen's arrest and that if the person is a felon, then the law will exculpate me?'

'What do you want from me? Seems to me that you know the legal niceties better than me. Yes, as I recollect, that is the law on it. But Mr Walters, Ben, let me speak as a friend. Don't do this thing. If you're looking for a quick death in your grief, then that's your business. Otherwise, leave it alone. You can't take on the whole, entire Kellerman Gang and expect to walk away with your life.'

'The law's as I stated it, though?'

The sheriff nodded glumly, looking harder at the man sitting in front of him. He noted for the first time the enormous horse pistol at Walters' hip and said wonderingly, 'You hope to brace Cade Kellerman and his cut-throats with an old cap and ball pistol? Man, they'll eat you alive. You're distracted. You don't know what you're doing. Why not return home and think things through a little first?'

'You're married, aren't you Grant?'

'I am.'

'What if somebody killed your wife? What would you do?'

'Same as you, I reckon. But you're missing the point. I don't give a tinker's cuss about Kellerman or any of his boys as you might kill. It's you I'm thinking of. You sure you ain't bit off more'n you can chew?'

Ben Walters smiled bleakly. 'Happen we'll have to see,' he said, 'But am I right about the law?'

'Right enough. But you'll find taking down Kellerman and his crew a hard row to hoe and no mistake.'

CHAPTER 4

It was surprising that with all the people busily engaged at that time in tracking down Cade Kellerman and claiming the bounty on his head, only two people, one an old man and the other little more than a boy, should have correctly gauged where he was likely to be heading. In retrospect though, it is not so difficult to understand. All the Indian trackers, bounty hunters, lawmen and Pinkertons agents were in hot pursuit of the Kellerman Gang and there didn't seem much point in trying to second-guess him. It was purely a matter of staying on his trail and waiting until they caught up with him. Had Cade Kellerman followed what everybody thought to be the sensible dodge and avoided towns, just keeping out in the wilderness, then it would indeed have been only a matter of time before he was run to earth. But a large part of the success of Kellerman and his boys lay in not doing what everybody expected. It was this that caused his men to stick with him, even when, as at Maple Bluff, they suffered the occasional reverse. So it was that on an unseasonably cold and wet day in late August, a party of riders entered Cedar Rapids, not as one noticeable and forbidding group of heavily armed men, but in ones and twos, with their rifles and carbines concealed where possible; covered in blankets and draped over with other gear.

Cade Kellerman entered the city first, riding alongside a 'breed called Jimmy Storm-cloud. Some said that he had acquired this strange name on account of he had been born during a thunderstorm; others that the Storm-cloud part of his name had been bestowed upon him as a child, due to his violent and unpredictable nature. The man himself did not invite questions of this sort and so he was likely to go to his grave with the puzzle of his name's origin unsolved. His skin was light enough for him to pass as white, but in his heart, he was pure Choctaw. He was the cruellest and most cunning of the men in Kellerman's gang, and for that reason their leader had what amounted almost to an affection for him. At any rate, he trusted and respected him and when Kellerman, as he infrequently did, required advice and counsel, it was to Jimmy that he turned. As they trotted towards the centre of town, Kellerman said, 'What do you say to this scheme? The truth now.'

The 'breed gave a sharp, humourless laugh. He said, 'You mean we have another choice?'

Kellerman shot him a sideways glance and said

admiringly, 'Meaning you don't like it, but since the alternative is getting caught and hanged, you'll go along of it for now?'

The other man grunted and said, 'Long as it ain't me you're fixin' for to sacrifice.'

'You don't care overmuch for Harker, do you?'

'Not a mite.'

'What of the others?

'Them neither.'

'There's your answer, then.'

The First National Bank of Iowa had its main office in Cedar Rapids, rather than Des Moines, for historical reasons that are nothing to the purpose of the present narrative. The fact was the biggest bank in Iowa was situated in Cedar Rapids and its vault was the repository for sacks full of silver coinage. As such, it might be thought that it would attract the attention of various criminal types, but it had not hitherto done so for two good reasons. The first of these was that the bank was guarded day and night by former members of the armed services, all of whom carried rifles and were proficient in their use. These men patrolled the street outside the bank, sat inside at night and were stationed atop of the roof. Most of these men were paid a pittance for their services, it being generally understood that the job was by way of being a sinecure, with very little risk attached to it. The chances of those guards ever having to hazard their lives to protect all that bullion were so slender as to be all but negligible.

The real protection of all those thousands and thousands of dollars' worth of silver stored in the basement of the bank in Cedar Rapids was something that any potential robber who gave the matter more than a few seconds thought would see at once, before turning regretfully from the lure of all that treasure. It was only because the men riding with Cade Kellerman were being hunted like game and in mortal fear of their lives that none of them had spotted the fatal flaw in any scheme to knock over the bank. Had they not been so harried and preoccupied with escaping the noose, they would have sat down quietly and figured the thing out for themselves. But then, they were in any case in the habit of allowing Cade Kellerman to do their thinking for them. He had chosen those men for their brutish natures and cold blood, rather than for the swiftness of their intellects.

The problem with stealing from the First National Bank of Iowa could be summed up in a single word: weight. Each of those silver dollars in the vault of the bank weighed one ounce; which meant, of course, that sixteen would amount to a pound. Assuming that twenty pounds in weight was about as much as you could stow comfortably in a saddle-bag, without slowing down your horse to an absolute crawl, then you would be making off with just $320. The tens of thousands of dollars in the vault might be a dazzling prospect, but unless you had a couple of ox carts to remove it, it was utterly safe. Robbing the bank of $10,000 would entail removing more than six hundredweight of coins.

If any of Kellerman's gang, other than Jimmy Storm-cloud, had set mind to this matter, then they might have realized that all this talk of taking out the bank in Cedar Rapids was no more than a puff of smoke and that Cade Kellerman's plans lay in another direction entirely.

Young Jackson had already worked out that there was no earthly chance of anybody making off with the silver held at the bank, but he still expected Kellerman and his men to fetch up in the town anyway. Even so, he was struck all of a heap when he glanced across the street and saw Cade Kellerman in person, riding along Main Street with another man. He almost felt like crying out to the passers-by, 'Look there, I was right all along. It's the famous Kellerman, large as life and twice as natural!' He restrained this impulse, which was perhaps just as well for him. Instead, he walked briskly along the sidewalk in the same direction as the two riders who, fortunately, were proceeding only at a leisurely trot.

In his jacket pocket, Abernathy Jackson had a litho of Kellerman's features, from a bill that had been distributed by the sheriff's office. It had evidently been copied from a photographic print, which made it a good likeness, but he could hardly pull this out in the street and compare it with the grim-visaged man who was heading, by the look of it, to the Metropole hotel; the very same place that Jackson himself was staying. As he hurried along after the two horsemen, he wondered at the fact that he was apparently the only man in the city who had spotted that the most wanted man in three states was riding openly through the streets. But there, how often do we actually look hard at strangers passing along the highway; let alone try and identify them as notorious malefactors?

Kellerman and his companion reined in outside the Metropole, dismounted and secured their horses to the hitching rail outside. Jackson hurried in after them. After all, he had a perfectly legitimate reason for being in such close proximity to the two men; he was staying in this hotel. As he approached the reception area, he found himself standing in line behind the men he had been following and was able to overhear the conversation that they were having with the clerk. Kellerman said, 'You have rooms free?'

'Yes, sir,' replied the clerk, 'We've a mort o' free rooms. You can, as they say, have your pick. You want two singles, a double, with or without a balcony, street view, rear view, second floor, third floor, with bathroom? Just say what you have in mind. Your wish is your command.'

Although he was doing his best not to attract unfavourable attention to himself while in town, Cade Kellerman could not forebear to remark to the fellow behind the counter, 'You talk a lot. Anybody ever tell you so?'

Not in the least out of countenance, the man answered, 'Well sir, you're not the first to make that same observation. It's a failing, I'll allow.'

Recollecting that he was trying not to make himself memorable in any way, Kellerman said, 'I guess we all have them, that is to say our failings. We'd like a double room, if you please, overlooking the street.'

At this point, Jimmy Storm-cloud said, 'Two single beds, mind.'

'Why yes,' said the clerk, 'I took that as read. You fellows in town for the convention, perhaps?'

'No,' said Kellerman, 'We've not come for any convention. Just passing through, you know.'

'Luggage?'

'No, but we'll pay cash now for two nights, if that's agreeable.'

After Kellerman and the man with him had taken their key and a boy had been summoned to show them to their room, Jackson asked the clerk for the key to his own room. His mind was working furiously as he went up the stairs to his room. He actually knew where Cade Kellerman, the man he had hoped to track down, was hiding out. It was beyond all belief that he should have been so successful, so fast. It was only now, that the first and what he had supposed to be the hardest part of his task had been undertaken, that Abernathy Jackson realized that he hadn't the faintest idea how he was next to proceed.

*

Sheriff Grant had insisted on having Ben Walters come over to his house for dinner that night. Not because he really thought that he would be able to dissuade him from the course of action upon which he had embarked, but simply out of common humanity. He thought that it would do Walters a power of good to be able to talk about his feelings. The problem about trying to talk the man out of riding the vengeance trail was that he, Charles Grant, would have ridden to the ends of the earth himself to track down and kill anybody who harmed his own family. He understood with perfect clarity what Ben Walters was about and, in his heart of hearts, thoroughly approved.

Miriam Grant was appalled to hear of the death of Mrs Walters and did her best to draw out the taciturn man and get him to talk about matters relating to his life. It was a pleasant enough meal and after spending those two nights out on the trail, it could not be denied that sitting at a table with good folk like these acted like a tonic on Ben Walters. After they had finished eating, the sheriff took Walters out onto the porch and invited him to sit awhile so that they could have a peaceful smoke. 'Miriam won't have it in the house,' Sheriff Grant admitted sheepishly. 'Imagine that, sheriff of the town and I can't do as I please in my own home. Well, that's marriage for you, I guess.' Then, feeling that this might have been a tactless remark, he said, 'I didn't mean nothing by that. It was stupid of me, after your loss and all.'

'It's nothing. I'm glad for you and your wife that you're so happy.'

'Seriously though, Mr Walters, what will you do if you catch up with Cade Kellerman? You really fixing for to kill him?'

'I don't know,' said Walters slowly, 'And that's God's honest truth. I killed men before, but that was in time o' war. You fought in the late War Between the States, I seem to recall?'

'That I did.'

'Well then, you know the way of it. When you're in battle and everybody around you is firing and falling dead, there's little enough time to weigh up the rights and wrongs of the thing. It's kill or be killed. I don't know if I'd kill a man in cold blood. I never done so in the whole course of my life.' Then, recollecting the boy he had lately shot, Walters amended the statement somewhat, by adding, 'Well, I only ever killed men when I was under the threat of death, at any rate.'

There was silence for a space and then Ben Walters spoke again. He said, 'I can't let that beast walk free, that much I know. I owe it to my dear wife to see justice done.'

A sudden and felicitous thought sprang into Sheriff Grant's mind and he said impulsively, 'If it's justice you're truly looking for, then why not put it on a proper, legal footing? I can swear you in as a deputy. Catch him and he'll hang for sure. That way, you won't have to do the job yourself.'

Walters said nothing, but stared out into the twilight. The sheriff didn't try and buffalo him; having set the idea out for consideration, he just left it for the other man to choose or reject, according to his own wishes. At length, Walters said, 'You have any authority in Cedar Rapids?'

Grant laughed and said, 'Not overly much. But if you've a warrant for Kellerman and take him to the law in Cedar Rapids, they'll be happy to let you bring him back here or even to Maple Bluff, if that's what you will. Kellerman's wanted in three states, you'd be spoiled for choice as to where you delivered him to be hanged.'

Ben Walters turned the proposition over in his mind. Sheriff Grant couldn't resist pointing out something that had already occurred to Walters. 'You'd not be foreclosing on the option of killing those bastards out of hand. You'd be in a stronger position if that's what you chose, 'cause you'd be the law.'

After a minute or so, Walters grunted and said, 'You're a wretch, Charles Grant, you know that? But you're right too. I was hot for shooting those men when I set out, but something happened on the road, it don't matter what, has put me off the idea of just shooting a man. I've an idea where I can lay hands on the leader of that band. You swear me in and I'll engage to bring him to justice, one way or another.'

Sheriff Grant got to his feet and said, 'You want to come down to my office now, I got all that's needful there.'

As they strolled through the town, Grant said, 'Sure you're up to the game? No offence meant.'

'None taken. I got no interest in anything now, other than seeing Cade Kellerman die. If I die in the attempt, well so be it.'

The casual way that this was said caused a shiver to run through Grant's body. He said curiously, 'You ain't seeking your own death, I suppose?'

'Can't say I'm troubled either way,' was the chilling reply.

When they reached the office, Grant opened the door and then lit a lamp. He invited Ben Walters to take a seat, while he sought the necessary paperwork. At last, having rooted around in a bureau that stood by the wall, he gave a cry of triumph. 'I knew I had it somewhere!' He smoothed out the crumpled sheet of paper and then walked over to where Walters was sitting and handed it to him. Both men had sombre expressions on their faces, for this was not a step to be lightly taken. The sheriff said, 'You resolved upon this?'

'I am.'

'Then you'd best stand and read aloud the words written there.'

Walters got to his feet and, staring hard at the sheet in the dim glow of the lamp, pronounced slowly, 'I, Benjamin Alexander Walters, do solemnly swear that I will perform with fidelity the duties of the office to which I have been appointed, and which I am about to assume. I do solemnly swear to uphold the constitution of the United States and to faithfully perform the duties of deputy sheriff for the state of Iowa. I further promise that I have not promised or given, nor will I give, any fee, gift, gratuity or reward for this office or for aid in procuring this office, that I will not take any fee, gift, or bribe, or gratuity for returning any person as a juror or for making any false return of any process and that I will faithfully execute the office of deputy sheriff to the best of my knowledge and ability, agreeably to law.'

When Walters had finished making this solemn declaration, Charles Grant said, 'I have witnessed your oath, this fourth day of September, in this year of grace eighteen hundred and seventy three.'

Neither of the men spoke for a while after the brief ceremony, which had been affecting in its simplicity, even being performed in the gloom of the dusty office, with only the two of them being present. Then Sheriff Grant broke the spell by opening a drawer of his desk, rummaging in it for a second or two and then taking out a small article made of pewter. This, he offered to Benjamin Walters, who took it in his hand and examined it, in the dim light of the flickering oil lamp. It was a six-pointed star, with tiny spheres on each point and inscribed with the words, 'DEPUTY SHERIFF'.

*

It was the second time that Cade Kellerman had laid plans to rid himself of a gang and make a fresh start. The first time he had done such a thing had been just three years after the War Between the States had drawn bloodily to its inevitable conclusion. At that time Kellerman, who had fought with Quantrill for the south, had been riding with a ruthless, rag-tag bunch of men who were, like him, former members of the Confederate army. They were not known then as the 'Kellerman Gang', but rather as the 'Missouri Holdfasts', on account that most of the men refused to accept that the war against the Yankees was really over. They thought of the robberies and other depredations that they undertook as being more like the continuation of the war, rather than as constituting ordinary criminal activity.

As the actions of the men with whom he rode became increasingly like guerilla warfare, the federal forces grew more and more ticked off with Kellerman and his one-time comrades in arms, until it seemed to him a matter of time before they were surrounded and killed in a gun battle with the army. Being, as he was, less devoted to the cause of the now dead Confederacy than he was to the very real cause of his own continued health and prosperity, Cade Kellerman decided that he would be well-advised to abandon his fellow bandits to the fate that would, in any case, surely overtake them before long. He helped organize a raid on a railroad depot and then informed the commander of the local garrison what was afoot. Kellerman was able to slip away, just before the troops arrived and sealed off the area. In the ensuing massacre, the men with whom Kellerman had been riding amply lived up to their name as 'diehards' or 'holdfasts'. They refused to surrender and in the course of the protracted gun battle, every one of them was killed, along with eleven federal soldiers.

After working alone for the best part of a twelvemonth, Cade Kellerman teamed up with a few other men and so was formed the nucleus of the outfit that would one day become known as the Kellerman Gang. Now though, the leader of this band of brigands and cutthroats was once more growing weary of the men he had hitched up with. Just as had been the case with his previous gang, Kellerman did not feel that it would be wise simply to walk away and abandon the men. There was no telling what men will say to save their own skins when cornered and he did not want to see anybody being offered the chance to turn state's evidence so that he could inform upon Kellerman in exchange for a greatly reduced sentence. Safer by far if the men were to be killed, rather than captured.

Cade Kellerman had been as vexed as anybody to find that wrecking that train had profited them nothing and served only to make them the target for every lawman, vigilante and bounty-hunter between here and the east coast, but there it was. The time had come to slip away and live quietly for a spell,

63

until the name of Kellerman had faded a little from memory. Before doing so though, he wished to ensure that none of those who had been riding with him were in any position to betray him in the future and the safest way of doing that was to engineer their deaths.

By a stroke of good fortune, Jack Harker, whose beard and face had been singed by Kellerman a short while previously, met his end without Cade Kellerman having to do anything at all to aid him on his way. This was the way of it.

Harker entered Cedar Rapids by himself and, after hitching his mount, went in search of some chewing tobacco. He had very little cash money in his pocket, but could still afford some tobacco; flavoured enticingly with rum. He was chewing a large wad of this substance and thoroughly enjoying it as he proceeded along the boardwalk. Finding that his mouth was just a little too full, Harker expectorated a stream of brown saliva, scarcely bothering to ensure that it went in the direction of the roadway. Most of it landed on the shin of a man who had just emerged from a nearby store. Harker looked up at once, meaning to apologise for his clumsiness, but was struck dumb by the extraordinary spectacle that this man presented. He exclaimed out loud and in the most tactless fashion imaginable, 'Lord a mercy, what in hell are you supposed to be, fella?'

There was some excuse for Harker's reaction to the unexpected sight of the man who stood glaring at him indignantly. This individual was outlandishly clad in the strangest garb Harker had ever set eyes on. He was wearing dark blue pants and a long, frock coat to match. On his head was perched a black derby, which sported a shiny brooch or something similar pinned to the front of it. Had it not been for the pistol, kept in a buttoned down dragoon holster at his hip, the fellow might have passed perhaps for an eccentrically dressed commissionaire or doorman at some fancy hotel. In fact, he was a police officer.

The previous year, the newly elected mayor of Cedar Rapids had visited New York and been vastly impressed with the costumes in which the police officers of that city were tricked out. He had resolved that as soon as possible, he would ensure that his own police force was similarly attired in a style that he thought very stylish, modern and up to date. Fully to understand the reaction of the officer upon whose leg Jack Harker had just spat a large quantity of saliva, mingled with tobacco juice, it is necessary to know two things.

In the first place, every single member of Cedar Rapids' police force loathed and abominated the fancy dress that the mayor had insisted they now wear. They thought, with some justification, that the blue frock coats and the derbies with the badge on the front made them figures of ridicule. The second thing to bear in mind is that the city's police force was riddled with corruption and most of the officers had rackets of one sort or another going on to enhance their meagre stipends. The fellow who Jack Harker had just run into had been shaking down a storekeeper, persuading him that a few dollars given each week to keep on the right side of the police might be a good investment for his future security. He had been working this racket with another officer, who was in the store setting out the precise details of this financial arrangement. To step out into the street and have somebody spit on his pants and then mock his appearance was sure to be the prelude to unpleasantness.

After Harker had asked him what the hell he was supposed to be, the policeman paused for a space before answering. Then he said, 'I'm supposed to be a police officer and you're under arrest for spitting on the sidewalk and treating a public official with contumely. Not to mention causing damage to this here clothing, which'll need to be replaced.' He reached under his coat and produced a pair of shiny handcuffs. 'Come on, we're going down to the office. Unless . . .'

'Unless what?' asked Harker.

' 'Less you shell out a fine this minute of twenty dollars.'

'Oh, it's like that, is it?' said Harker, catching the drift, 'It's a shakedown.'

The other man shrugged and said, 'Call it what you will. Let's have the money. It's that or fourteen days in the cells.'

It was those final words, thrown in so casually,

which signed the death warrants of two men. Jack Harker had barely enough to pay for a few nights in a flophouse and he wasn't about to part with that. If he were to be locked up for a few weeks, as this fellow was suggesting, it would not only mean missing out on the silver robbery, but there was an excellent chance that somebody might identify him as one of the Kellerman Gang being hunted far and wide, across the entire state. It wasn't to be thought of. He said to the policeman, 'Why'n't we step into this alley and do business?'

This was all working out as the crooked officer had hoped. His partner was still in the store, collecting their first payment and presumably making the necessary arrangements for the future. Now he himself had made twenty dollars in a matter of seconds. Things were looking up that day. He followed his latest mark into the space between two buildings and watched eagerly as the man reached into his clothing to find the money. He hardly had time to stare in amazement as, instead of the expected bills, the rough-looking fellow pulled out a thin-bladed knife from somewhere and plunged it into the police officer's chest. The wounded man looked stupidly at his assailant, began pondering a response to the assault and then dropped dead on the spot; the knife having gone clean through his heart.

For Jack Harker, killing a lawman in this way was just one of those things you did when you were cornered, but the dead man's partner took a quite different view of the matter when he emerged from the store, whose owner he had been menacing, and saw his fellow officer disappearing down an alleyway. He arrived just in time to see the other officer fall lifeless in the dirt and actually saw the bloody knife in the hands of a man who was clearly the killer. Although a renowned man of action, Harker was for a moment taken aback to find a policeman coming across him in the very act of murder. Although he paused only for the merest fraction of a second before going for the gun at his hip, it was long enough to give his opponent the edge. The man's pistol was clear of its holster in no time and before Jack Harker had time to consider things further, a ball took him in the shoulder. He staggered back, frantically trying to keep his balance, and the second one struck him squarely in the middle of his breast-bone; killing him almost instantly as the splinters of bone were driven into his heart. When the echoes died down, there were two corpses lying in the cramped space between the two buildings.

CHAPTER 5

For Abernathy Jackson, a great deal was hanging on bringing Kellerman and his band to justice. And did he even want them to be brought to justice? Was that in truth the object of the exercise? If he simply walked down the road and told the local law here in Cedar Rapids where they could lay hands on Cade Kellerman, would that stand him in good stead with Pinkerton? Perhaps not; the old man had specifically asked for Jackson to bring him 'intelligence' or information. Would handing over this famous bandit to the police count or did Mr Pinkerton mean intelligence that would do his company some good? Jackson had a sneaking suspicion that it was this latter that the founder and head of the Pinkertons outfit had had in mind. For his own part, Jackson knew that he was less concerned with justice in the abstract than he was with self-advancement. Helping to catch this villain was about doing Abernathy

Jackson a bit of good, rather than protecting inno-
cent folk from the depredations of a dangerous
bandit.

After mulling this matter over in his mind, while
he sat with a coffee in the dining room attached to
the hotel, Jackson had an absolute brainwave. He
jumped to his feet and went over to the fellow who
was wiping down the tables in a desultory and bored
manner. 'Say, you've lived in this town a while, I
guess?'

'Only my whole life long!' replied the young man
gloomily, 'Like to die here and all, less'n something
happens.'

'Tell me though, is there an office of the
Pinkertons agency in Cedar Rapids?'

'Sure there is. Well, there's a fellow who works for
'em. He runs an office down the way a bit, nigh to the
Methodist church. Name of Carter. Why, what's
afoot?'

'Nothing to speak of, I was just curious is all.'

The odd look that the other man gave him suggested to Jackson that this explanation was not
accepted at face value, but this didn't bother him
overly much. He went back to his table, gulped down
the remains of his coffee and left the hotel to find
the local Pinkertons office.

The Pinkerton's National Detective Agency was
such a vast enterprise at that time that most cities and
large towns had a representative of some kind.
Sometimes this was a full-time worker employed by

Pinkertons, in smaller places it was often a man who had some other line of work and held a commission from Pinkertons to be ready and able to lend a hand when required. Such men were always on the lookout for useful information that they could feed back to the head office in Chicago. When a young man walked into the office of Pete Carter that fine sunny morning, that individual was delighted to hear that something was happening thereabouts.

Carter ran a small printing firm and was employed by Pinkertons chiefly to pass on anything of note to their head office. He dreamed, though, of making a name for himself and being engaged to run a Pinkertons office in some big city. When Abernathy Jackson told him that he had some information that he wished to send to Mr Pinkerton himself in Chicago, Peter Carter saw an opportunity to do himself some good.

'Information for the chief, hey?' said Carter. 'I guess I'm the one to do that for you. What is it? What's to do?'

Young he might have been, but Abernathy Jackson wasn't a perfect fool and saw at once that the sharp-faced man in front of him would most likely be seeking credit for himself for anything told him. He said slowly, not wishing to appear rude, 'The information I have is for Mr Pinkerton alone. Do you have some secure channel of communication, a special telegraph line or something?'

'Special telegraph? Case you hadn't noticed son,

we're in Cedar Rapids, not New York City! I'll engage to get a message to head office, but it'll be going through the regular system. Don't worry, I'll be sure to mention your name though.'

'You couldn't let me have the telegraphic address of the head office and so on, I suppose? Then I wouldn't need to trouble you at all, I could send the message for my own self.'

Pete Carter's eyes narrowed and he said sharply, 'And a fine sort of fool I'd look, if you go running to the old man with news about something right here in town that I know nothing about! Don't think it for a moment. No, I aim to be in on anything of the sort, you may depend upon that.'

'Then I guess I'll be leaving it for now. Sorry to have troubled you, sir.'

As he headed back to the hotel, Jackson wondered why he had not thought to establish during his interview with Mr Pinkerton just exactly how he was supposed to relay this intelligence that the old man had asked him to acquire.

Once Kellerman had come up with his plan, which was in any case something he had had in mind for just this sort of occasion, it had been absurdly easy to execute. He had led his men up onto the rocky flank of a hill, a place that was criss-crossed with little brooks and streams. Then he said to them, 'Time to split up in different directions. This rocky country'll make tracking the devil of a job. Anyways, we can't proceed further like this, with all of us riding side by side. We all head off now across streams and any other water, then head hell for leather all over the place. After a mile or two, we make for Cedar Rapids. With good fortune, they won't be able to track any one of us.'

So it had proved, because after following the clear trail of a dozen men on horseback, the trackers were at a loss to know how to react when this deep, clear track suddenly split up into individual riders. Those riders were cunning and resourceful men, desirous of not having their necks stretched, and so they had a great incentive to ride hard, in and out of water, across rock, doubling back on their tracks and using every other trick in the trade to throw off pursuit. In this, they were successful, and not one of them was caught. Before parting, Kellerman had given instructions for their rendezvous in Cedar Rapids, which would not, if he had anything to do with it, entail the whole gang appearing together on the streets of the city and so attracting attention to themselves.

The day after he and Jimmy Storm-cloud booked into the Metropole, Kellerman went for a little ride by himself. He bore no particular animosity or ill will to the band of men with whom he had been riding, on and off, for the last few years. They had had some good times together, but the fact was that they were now a liability. After the fiasco at Maple Bluff, every man jack of them were marked men and there was no counting on their loyalty. A man who has been captured and is in jeopardy of his very life will say literally anything to escape the shadow of the noose. Any one of those comrades of his might try and turn state's evidence and betray him. Safer by far if the whole boiling lot of them were to be safely under the ground!

Cade Kellerman had figured out how he was to rid himself permanently of a dozen or so men. He would need something uncommon to do so, which accounted for his trip out of Cedar Rapids that morning. He was on his way to meet a man called Patrick Carstairs, who was known by one and all for some miles around not by his given name, but rather by the soubriquet of 'the nitro man'.

For centuries, the only explosive known to humankind was gunpowder. Then, in 1847, an Italian chemist called Ascanio Sobrero discovered quite by chance that combining nitric acid with glycerine in the right proportions and under the right conditions would produce an explosive far more powerful than ordinary black powder. For the next twenty years, those quarrying stone, digging tunnels and wells or building railroads through mountains found that nitroglycerin, as the new compound was christened, was an absolute godsend. There was one great drawback, however, and this was that the new explosive was enormously sensitive to being mishandled. One could throw a barrel of gunpowder off a wagon and it was no more dangerous than sawdust or sugar. Nitroglycerin, on the other hand, could be detonated by something as trivial as a sharp knock to the container in which it was held. Worse still, it had an alarming tendency to degrade spontaneously, until it was prone to explode just because the temperature rose or fell by a couple of degrees.

Nineteen years after the invention of nitroglycerin, the Central Pacific Railroad decided to use a huge quantity of the stuff to blast a tunnel through the Sierra Nevada mountains in order to link California with Nevada by a direct railroad service. They had the explosives delivered in the first instance by stagecoach to the San Francisco office of Wells Fargo. When the consignment arrived there on April 9th 1866, it received an unexpected jolt as the crate of glass containers was being carried into the storage room. The resulting explosion demolished the entire building, as well as killing fifteen people.

The San Francisco incident prompted California to pass a law forbidding the transportation of nitroglycerin along any of the highways or railroads in the whole state. Other states soon passed similar laws, which meant that any company or private individual wishing to use nitroglycerin was obliged to have it made at the site where it would be used. This gave rise to an illicit trade in nitro and caused men such as Patrick Carstairs to set up little laboratories, like moonshine stills, to manufacture nitroglycerin for those who merely wanted to acquire a gallon or two and do without the fuss and expense of hiring a man to travel to where they were working and make it on the spot.

The cabin and ramshackle barn adjacent to it put Cade Kellerman strongly in mind of a moonshiner's abode. It was situated by the side of a little stream, for chemists, like moonshiners, need a ready supply of running water. As he approached the place, a man with a long black beard emerged from the barn with a scattergun cradled in his arms. He must have heard the hoofbeats or jingling of harness, for he looked ready for any eventuality. Kellerman said, 'You'll not need that cannon of your'n.'

'Happen I'll be the judge o' that,' said the man, with the shotgun still pointing vaguely in Kellerman's direction. 'What's your business here?'

'Nothin' as'll need weaponry, be assured. I want to buy your wares.'

The man peered closely at the other, as if trying to gauge whether or not he might be an agent of the state, determined to arrest him for the illegal manufacture and transportation of high explosives. Evidently, he made up his mind that Cade Kellerman was a horse of another colour, for he lowered his weapon and said briefly, 'Come into m'house. We don't need to discuss business out here in the open.'

The 'house' was a one-room shack, with a bed in one corner and a table set in the middle. A few shelves held various pots, pans, sacks of meal and suchlike. Presumably the synthesizing of nitroglycerin was conducted in the barn, where, Kellerman imagined, the fellow must have set up his manufactory.

'Take a seat,' said the nitro man, 'And tell me what you're after.'

'That's easily stated. Two gallon o' nitro.'

'You an engineer?'

'I reckon as that's my affair,' said Kellerman shortly, 'You have the thing for sale, I want to buy it.'

It was clear that Patrick Carstairs was used to having his own way and not being brushed off like that, because he said, 'It's my business if aught happens and a man dies. I'll have those idiot police from Cedar Rapids crawling round here in next to no time. I don't want anything I sell being used within a few miles of here. Why d'you want nitro and where'll you be using of it?'

'Ah, it's no big secret. I've a farm, over the other side of Cedar Rapids, twenty miles from here. There's a reef of rock blocking me from one field. I have to ride all round it to get to my pasture. I want to blast a little gully, as a short cut, you mind. There, does that satisfy?'

'I reckon,' said Carstairs. 'Come out to the barn and I'll show what I have.'

The barn was full of retorts, glass tubing, bubbling vats and serried rows of earthenware jars, which presumably held the finished product. It looked for all the world like a moonshiner's set-up. Kellerman exclaimed admiringly, 'Why, you've a regular science laboratory here. I am truly impressed.' He spoke so

77

fulsomely because a new idea had struck him on the walk from the cabin to the barn and he was feeling enchanted with his own cleverness. That being so, he could afford to be pleasant to the other fellow.

Carstairs grunted and replied, 'You'll be wanting two of them there demijohns. There's a gallon in each. That's a total of twenty pounds' weight for two.'

'I know the weight of it,' said Kellerman, 'Which is why I said I wanted two.'

'Well, come back to the house and you can give me the cash. I like to handle money in private, you know.'

The two men left the barn and headed towards the little tumbledown shack that the nitro man dignified with the name of 'house'. Cade Kellerman was something of a traditionalist, at least where firearms were concerned. He preferred a cap and ball pistol any day of the week to one of the more up-to-date models with self-contained brass cartridges. He accordingly sported an old, single-action Navy Colt at his hip, which gave him a slightly old-fashioned and faintly quaint air. Just as the two of them reached Carstairs' home, Cade Kellerman stepped back slightly to allow his host to open the door of his home. This meant that the nitro man had his back to Kellerman and consequently did not notice that he had drawn his pistol.

As he lifted the latch, in order to open the door, Patrick Carstairs fancied that he heard a faint, metallic click. He half turned, to see what might have caused the sound, but before he could look round, there was a deafening roar and Carstairs had the impression that he had been punched very hard in the back. He staggered and there was a second crash. This time, he felt a blow to his head and then nothing more; he fell to the ground, stone dead.

When he first came to visit the nitro man, Kellerman had it in mind to hold him up at gunpoint and then steal a couple of gallons of nitroglycerin from his stores. Having seen the thirty gallons or so that Carstairs had stockpiled in the barn, gave Cade Kellerman another idea entirely. There must be the better part of a quarter ton of explosives in that barn. He had planned to lure his men to some lonely spot and then blow them to hell with two gallons, or twenty pounds, of nitro. The weak point about the plan was that, depending upon how close they stood together, there was always the chance that one or two might survive the explosion and that would never do. If, however, the men were milling around in the vicinity of not twenty pounds but two or three hundred pounds of nitroglycerin, the chances of there be any survivors after the blast would be vanishingly small. It was this realization that had sealed Patrick Carstairs' fate.

A quick glance around suggested that nobody had witnessed the nitro man's death and so Kellerman pulled open the door and dragged the corpse into the cramped little hut. If he was any judge of such things, this was a man who was often coming and going and whose absence for a day or two would not be in any way remarkable. Those who visited this spot were, in any case, proposing to undertake an illegal act, which is to say transporting nitroglycerin along a public road. Nobody had an incentive for advertising his presence here. Nonetheless, it would not be wise to alert any casual visitor to the presence of a corpse here, particularly one which its head blown half off.

Cade Kellerman manhandled the late Patrick Carstairs until he was lying snugly beneath his bed. Once the blanket had been artistically draped over the edge of the bed, so as to conceal the body, there was no reason for anybody to suspect that foul play had taken place here. The area immediately outside the cabin was liberally splashed with blood and brain matter, so Kellerman spent a few minutes kicking dirt around, until it would be all but impossible for anybody to tell that a man had died violently here not thirty minutes since.

Notwithstanding the fact that he had nerves of steel, Kellerman felt a little uneasy about handling nitroglycerin. He had seen ample evidence of the effect of the substance on the human frame during the war. One time, he had come upon the aftermath of a transport, consisting of a mule carrying two five-gallon carboys of nitro. There had been four men escorting the mule along a track, but all that remained of the party was a hole about three-feet deep in the sandy loam. As to the men and the mule, you would have been hard-pressed to gather up enough flesh and bone to fill up a pint pot. They had been blown, quite literally, into pieces. That was a hundredweight; there must be at least two or three times as much in the nearby barn.

Very gingerly, Kellerman picked up one of the earthenware vessels that apparently contained nitro and, walking very slowly and carefully, he carried it out of the barn and placed it at the back wall of the barn, where it would not be seen from the path leading to the nitro man's place of business. Then he went back into the barn and took another of the demijohns and repeated the process, setting it next to its fellow. Then he collected a few pieces of brush-wood and concealed the brown, glazed jars. Only a few wooden boards separated them now from the bulk of the explosives stored in the barn.

Once he had accomplished this task, Kellerman breathed a little easier. He found to his disgust that beads of sweat were running down his face like tears. He had been that nervous of some mishap. Facing men in a shooting match was one thing; for such a thing he was utterly without nerves. This though was another matter. He shook his head irritably. Maybe he was getting too old for lively games such as this?

All was now quite ready. It was only necessary to persuade his men to meet him here and then make sure that he was concealed at some good distance with his carbine. A single shot slamming into one of those jars of nitro would set it off, and its companion besides. This would in turn trigger the large quantity of explosives in the barn, something like a third of a ton by Kellerman's reckoning. Anybody within fifty or a hundred feet of the place would be killed for certain-sure.

CHAPTER 6

Ben Walters had found it even easier than Abernathy Jackson to figure out where Cade Kellerman and his boys were most likely to fetch up. He had, after all, been more than once in a precisely similar situation; that is to say on the lam and desperately anxious to save his neck. He had in those circumstances, whenever possible, headed for the largest town or city he could reach. It is a damned sight easier to lose yourself in a city than it is out in some remote and uninhabited area.

It had been some years since Ben Walters had been to Cedar Rapids. When last he had visited the town, it had been a pretty sleepy sort of place. Now, it was a bustling hive of activity. As he trotted the mare along the road that ran from the railroad depot to the Metropole hotel, Walters wondered what the chances were of running Kellerman and his boys to earth in such a large and lively town; a town getting so big now that they would most likely be applying for recognition as a city before long. When he reached the Metropole, Walters dismounted, looped the reins of his horse around the hitching post and then passed through the bat-wing doors into the imposing building.

The ground floor of the Metropole was essentially a classy saloon and dining room. This brought in the great bulk of the hotel's income, for sometimes there would be no guests at all in the upper four floors, but even during such lean spells there was never any shortage of men wishing to eat and drink at the Metropole.

'Good morning to you, sir,' said the clerk, in an affable tone of voice, 'Are you looking for a room or a reservation in our dining hall?'

'I'd like a room, please. Are you at all crowded?'

'Oh, you know. Fair to middling, fair to middling.'

Walters did not feel that it was yet time to tip his hand and show anybody in Cedar Rapids his star. There might come a point where such a move would be advantageous, but there was no point in lying down before he was called to do so. He booked a room for two nights, paying up front in cash.

After checking over the room, Walters took the mare across to a livery stable that he had marked as he entered town. He then found an eating house and had a hearty breakfast. While he ate, Ben Walters tried to cast his mind back a quarter of a century and asked himself, 'What would I do, if I had just screwed up a robbery and had every lawman in three states on my tail?' In the first instance, of course, he would try and lose any pursuers. Having done so, then he would most likely have tried to make up for the disappointment of the bungled robbery and see if he could not pick up a little money in the town to which he had fled. Having done so, he would then have bolted again and made tracks as fast as he was able to his own home, assuming that he had one. Knowing how the minds of men like that worked, Walters guessed that after the failure of the ambush of the railroad train, they would now be red hot keen to make up for it by hitting somewhere pretty quickly. Before leaving the place where he'd just broken his fast, he went over to the fellow serving food and said with a straight face, 'Listen, if I was wanting to commit a robbery in this town, where would you recommend I begin?'

This whimsical approach apparently touched the counterman's humour, for he replied gravely, 'Well sir, I might suggest the First National Bank, which is situated down the way a little, nigh to the depot. I believe that they have plenty of silver and gold on the premises, such as would satisfy the most rapacious of robbers.'

Walters chuckled at that. 'Seriously though,' he said, 'Do you have any robberies hereabouts, other than the usual, run-of-the-mill thefts from shops and such?'

'I don't mind that any bandits and so on have yet

favoured us with their attentions in this town, least-ways, not for a good few years. If you care to step down the street and cast your eye over the bank, I've an idea that you might see why that is.' The man leaned a little closer and said, lowering his voice, 'Is something afoot? I kind of get the idea that if you're not the law, then you're next door to it.'

'It's nothing to fret about. I'm just keeping a weather eye on one or two things is all.'

After taking his leave of the counterman, Walters made his way in the direction of the First National. Before he even reached it, he caught a glimpse of a uniformed figure, holding a rifle and standing guard behind the parapet around the roof of a stout, white-painted building. As he came closer he saw that, as he had suspected, these were the premises of the First National Bank of Iowa. Another uniformed guard was patrolling the bank at street level, march-ing around like a military sentry with a rifle held in his arms. It was impressive and, even though it had been twenty-five years since he had done anything dishonest, Ben Walters stopped for a moment and considered how he would go about stealing from the bank.

The difficulty was, of course, that this was a busy, civilized place with a well-organized police force. There was an army base too, not more than a few hours' ride away. Across the road was the railroad depot and that seemed to Walters to give a good opportunity. Take out the telegraph line leading from town in the same direction and alongside of the railroad; that would be the first step. Then, once you'd got the gold, silver or cash money from the bank, seize a locomotive at the depot and simply drive it off at top speed. When you'd got a good distance, then send the thing on by itself, with the throttle jammed open. That way, nobody would know where you'd jumped train.

As he stood there, mulling over the way that he would knock over the First National Bank, were he still to be on the scout, Ben Walters was suddenly overcome by the absurdity of the thing. He shook his head and, for the first time since the death of his wife, a smile appeared on his lips. It was instantly extinguished, but Walters was aware that he was still, despite his crushing grief, able to smile. He did not know whether this was a comfort to him or rather a betrayal of his dead wife.

A flash of light caught Walters' attention. It seemed to come from high in the sky and he glanced up curiously to see what might have caused it. Then there was another, less noticeable, wink and he realized that it was something up on a rooftop near the bank; something glassy that was reflecting sunlight down into the street. He'd take oath that there was a man with field glasses up on that roof, most likely spying out the bank.

Casually, without any appearance of undue haste, Walters sauntered across the street and made his way to the back of the building where he'd seen the flashes of reflected sunlight. If somebody was staking out the bank, then this might be his first line on the Kellerman Gang. After screwing up the train robbery, it was a racing certainty that they would be on the prowl for some other target now and what better than a big bank in a prosperous city?

A ladder, which Walters supposed to be a rudimentary fire escape, was bolted to the brickwork and ran up the back of the building, alongside the windows. It continued past the window on the third floor, leading right up to the flat roof. This must surely be how whoever was up on that roof had gained access to his vantage point.

About halfway to the roof, Walters had to stop and catch his breath. He surely was getting too old for games of this kind! When he finally reached roof level, he peered cautiously over the edge of the roof and saw a man lying flat, training a pair of field glasses on the nearby bank. It was just exactly as he had suspected; the bank was being staked out, with a view to knocking it over. The fellow had his back to Walters and seemed in any case wholly occupied with what he was observing through his glasses. Very carefully, he clambered onto the lead-covered roof and began moving quietly towards the prone figure. Walters intended to jump the fellow from behind and perhaps club him into submission by cracking his head with the horse pistol hanging at his waist. But, as the saying goes, 'Man proposes, but God disposes'. He was within a dozen feet of his target when one of the boards lying beneath the lead sheeting of the roof creaked. Then things happened very quickly indeed.

The man lying on the roof whirled round and his hand snaked down as he presumably went for a gun. As Ben Walters tried to pull out his own pistol, he found that in the course of climbing up the ladder, one corner of his jacket had somehow become entangled with the hammer of the revolver. That fact, combined with the extraordinary weight of the weapon itself, caused a fatal moment of delay as he struggled to jerk the thing from its holster. By the time he'd freed it, cocking the piece with his thumb as he did so, Walters found that the other man had a gleaming, nickel-plated pistol of his own out and that it was pointing, as far as he was able to gauge, straight at his heart. He still had not raised his own weapon and it occurred to him that it would be a very unwise move, at this stage of the proceedings, to do so. There was, he supposed, still a remote chance that matters would end peaceably, but he was very much inclined to doubt it. In all likelihood, this was going to turn out just exactly as anybody could have predicted from the very beginning, with an old fool being gunned down by an agile, ruthless and trigger-happy youngster.

Earlier that day, Abernathy Jackson had arisen for breakfast, only to find that Cade Kellerman had left town at first light and that nobody knew if or when he would be returning. Jackson gleaned this information while eavesdropping on a private conversation between the 'breed that Kellerman had booked into the Metropole with and the clerk behind the counter at the reception area. It was a bitter blow and Jackson could not help but wonder if he would not have done better to trust the fellow to whom he had spoken the previous day, who was representing the Pinkertons agency in the town.

'Your friend left mighty early this morning,' observed the clerk, 'Mighty early. I hope there's nothing amiss?'

Jimmy Storm-cloud eyed the man with contempt and said, 'What's it to you when he comes and goes? We paid up for last night and this'n. You don't stand to lose if the two of us dig up and leave town this minute. You got your money.'

'No offence meant, I'm sure. Merely making conversation.'

'Well, don't!' replied the 'breed emphatically, 'I don't take to it.' Without another word, he stalked from the lobby, evidently put out.

'Lordy,' said the clerk to Jackson, who was waiting to ask about the location of certain stores in Cedar Rapids, 'Ain't some folk touchy though?'

'You think he has something to hide?'

'Ain't we all?' replied the clerk, his attention already turning to other matters. 'Is there aught I can help you with?'

'Why yes. Do you know where I might acquire such

an item as a pair of field glasses? Binoculars, you know.'

The man rubbed his chin meditatively and said, 'You might try Weizmann's, down the road away. Same side of the street as us, going the opposite direction to the railroad depot.'

After he had eaten breakfast, Jackson wandered down the street in the direction the hotel clerk had told him. Sure enough, there was a little store that specialised in all sorts of odds and ends; including eyeglasses and binoculars. The owner was happy to produce a variety for Abernathy Jackson to inspect at his leisure, saying, 'If you want something to be able to carry conveniently, then these might suit.' He indicated a compact pair of field glasses; made of brass and finished with Morocco leather of the kind with which the more expensive kind of book is bound. Jackson fell in love with these and, after picking them up and hefting them in his hand, determined that they were the very thing.

'How much are these?' he asked casually. The owner of the store was not deceived by the offhand way in which the question had been asked and could see at once that the young man had set his heart on the beautifully crafted article.

'Truth is,' said Mr Weizmann, 'Those might be a little out of your price range. They're small, but the craftsmanship is exquisite. Mayhap you'd be better off with something a little less dear.' Having said this, Weizmann observed with satisfaction the indignation in the boy's face and the slight reddening of his cheeks at the suggestion that he could not afford something in the little store.

A little stiffly, Jackson said, 'I'll be the best judge of what might within my means, sir. How much are these glasses?'

'Well,' said the little man, with every appearance of reluctance, 'They cost thirty dollars. Mind, I have other pairs every bit as good for less than that. . . .'

'I'll take them.'

When the sale had been completed and the owner of Weizmann's Sundries was rubbing his hands together in glee at rooking a gullible young fool, Abernathy Jackson was strolling thoughtfully down main street in the direction of the depot. Although he himself had already done the necessary calculations tending towards the weight of silver bullion, he had a notion that the First National Bank was still going to play a part in his hunt for the Kellerman Gang.

Since Cade Kellerman himself was gone, the Lord knew where, it seemed to Jackson that setting an unobtrusive watch upon the bank might help to identify others of the gang who might be in town. He already knew of one of them; the half-breed who was also staying at the Metropole, but it was a fair guess that there were others in Cedar Rapids. Was the plan to knock over the bank? Or had they just come here to escape from the dogged pursuit that had begun shortly after the massacre at Maple Bluff? For want of a better plan, Jackson figured that he might as well find a convenient spot and watch those who showed any special interest in the building that housed the First National Bank of Iowa. So it was that he found a route up onto a nearby rooftop and then settled down that morning, simply to keep an eye on the bank and its environs.

The situation could hardly have been more tense, with one man pointing a gun at another, whose own gun was drawn and ready to be brought up to aim. Ben Walters, for all that he had expected to find a desperate bandit perched up on the roof, found instead that he was facing a well-dressed young fellow who could not be more than twenty years of age. More than that, this youngster had an honest and open face. Shrewd and determined, by the look of him, it was true, but Walters would have taken oath that this was no ruthless killer. He said in a quiet and reassuring tone of voice, 'Listen, why don't you and I lay down our weapons and talk. Strikes me, there's some misunderstanding here.'

Abernathy Jackson may have looked like a harmless soul to Ben Walters' eye, but that was not how Walters himself appeared to Jackson. The young man saw a grim, grizzled and unshaven man in his riper years, waving a pistol about. Walters had been travelling rough since leaving his home and nobody looking at him now would imagine in a thousand years that this tough-looking character was really a

Justice of the Peace, regular church-goer and governor of an orphans' asylum. In truth, he looked every inch a desperado who was likely to stick at nothing. Jackson said, 'Lay down my gun? I don't think it for a moment. I know your boss was in town last night.'

'My boss? I don't rightly understand you,' said Walters slowly. Then his voice quickened, as he suddenly realized what this boy was driving at. He said, 'You looking for the same man as me?'

'I didn't say I was looking for anybody.'

'Listen here,' said Ben Walters, his interest piqued, 'I'm going to lay down my gun here. I'll move slow as you like, but maybe then we can talk.' Very carefully, thinking how absurd it would be to meet his death up here on the top of a building, he set his pistol down and then moved back from it and raised his hands to indicate his pacific intentions. 'There now,' he said, 'I think we're on the same track. You're no robber. Judging by the way you speak and dress, I'd say you're from out east somewhere. Educated too, by the sound of it. Boston? New York? Why don't I set down here and you tell me what's afoot?'

All the while, Abernathy Jackson watched the older man with the greatest caution, ready for any sign of treachery. He didn't really know what he would do if the other fellow dived for his pistol, but there seemed to be no sign of such a thing happening presently.

Jackson had managed to wriggle around, so that

he was now sitting on his haunches and separated from the man he had supposed to be a member of the Kellerman Gang by about ten or twelve feet. He said, 'Well who are you then? If you're not a bandit.'

'I'm a sheriff,' was the surprising answer. 'Justice of the Peace as well, away over in Maple Bluff.'

'Maple Bluff? You mean where the train. . . .'

'That's right,' said Ben Walters grimly. 'The self-same place where Kellerman and his boys wrecked the train. I'm pursuing them.'

It struck Jackson that he was very much mistaken about what was going on here and he replaced the shiny little revolver in the holster that fitted under his left armpit. 'Are you here officially?' he asked, looking crestfallen. 'I thought I was the only one who knew where they'd fetched up.'

'It's by way of being a long story, son. Why don't we make our way down that ladder and find somewhere we can have a cup or two of strong coffee. Happen this meeting might work to our mutual advantage, so to speak.'

It had taken some time to allay Abernathy Jackson's suspicions, but after he had heard everything that Walters said, he was fully convinced. For his part, Ben Walters marvelled at the way in which this boy had succeeded in tracking down the most wanted man in three states purely by exercising his cerebral powers and with no previous experience in either breaking or enforcing the law. The two of them were sitting in a secluded corner of an all but deserted eating house in a minor street, well away from both the bank and the depot. Walters said, 'We won't fall out over this, son. You want to persuade old man Pinkerton that you've the brains to find such a wanted man, I can help you do it. But you have to see that Kellerman himself is mine. I don't aim for to see anybody else take him down but me.'

Jackson did not know whether to be pleased and relieved or angry and frustrated. On the one hand, he hadn't the faintest idea how to go about tackling Kellerman and his gang now that he had found them, but on the other he did not want to be robbed of the glory for capturing the man. He said, 'I don't see that, Mr Walters. Which is to say, how I'll get the credit, but at the same time, you get to take Cade Kellerman.'

'Why boy, did you never read in scripture where we are told to be as cunning as serpents, but as gentle as doves? Here's the way of it. I'll help you get word to Pinkertons, telling that the gang is here in town. Then, just as the Pinkerton boys come racing in, they'll find themselves pipped at the post by me. That way, old mister Pinkerton will know that you brought him gold dust in the way of intelligence about wrongdoers and you get the credit of it. I get what I want too, which is a reckoning with the man who killed my wife.'

'You're forgetting though, like I told, I've no way of contacting Mister Pinkerton directly.'

'I didn't forget that. I can help you there, if you

will. I know just exactly how we can get a message through to the old man.'

Partly as a consequence of his once having been a bandit himself and also because in his later years he had been appointed a Justice of the Peace, Ben Walters had maintained a lively interest in law-keeping over a period in excess of a quarter century. This had led to his keeping up to date with various matters that did not directly affect him, but in which he had a personal interest. One of these subjects was private agencies. He had entertained at his home more than one private policeman and knew a fair bit about the operations of agencies such as Pinkertons. In particular, he had learned how the various Pinkertons men communicated with their offices, using the ordinary telegraph system to convey the most sensitive and confidential information.

'You have pen and paper at hand?' asked Walters.

'I have a notebook.'

'Well then, let's set to and get word to that fellow who you're wanting a job offer from.'

Pinkertons used a simple cipher to send their urgent messages back to Chicago. Such telegrams were apt to be wordy and so expensive. This meant that they were not used lightly, as the thrifty head of the Pinkertons Agency retained all his Scots reluctance to part with unnecessary money. But in emergencies, the code used was an effective one. It consisted of making every third word of a message the important ones and the others just fillers.

Whenever an incomprehensible telegram was received, it went straight up to Mister Pinkerton himself. This is the message, as it was composed by the two men:

PLEASE SEND COLOUR CHARTS. OUR MAN WHO IS IN CONTACT SAYS CEDAR GREEN IS RAPID NEW LINE. STAYING IN TOWN AT THE OLD METROPOLE.

'That ought to do the trick,' said Walters, 'Colour man in Cedar Rapid staying at Metropole. It wouldn't do to put Kellerman's name in a telegram, but they'll twig that, soon as somebody reads it out loud. Old Pinkerton's no fool.'

'When ought we to send it?' asked Jackson, feeling that control of things had slipped somehow from his grasp and hoping to establish that he was still needing to be consulted. 'Will we have time to nail Kellerman before the men from Pinkertons get here?'

'It's two hundred and fifty miles as the crow flies, from here to Chicago. I'm guessing that as soon as this is read, they'll be despatching a bunch of men, strong enough to settle Kellerman and all his boys. You know that Pinkerton commandeers whole entire trains at need? He rides high, that one.'

'It'll be my name on the telegram? He'll know as it was I who tipped him the wink?'

'Lord a mercy,' exclaimed Ben Walters irascibly, 'I

want no part in the business, if that's what you're thinking of. It will be enough for me to see that villain hanged or shot, whichever is worse for him.'

'You're still planning to kill him your own self, like you said? Or when you talk of hanging, that mean you'd be happy to see him arrested now?'

'Nothing about this affair is apt to make me happy, as you put it. As to whether I will kill him myself, I don't know. It's enough for you and me to hunt him down and then see what chances. You ever hear of that cookery book which recommends that you "Take your hare, when once it is caught" as the beginning of a recipe for jugged hare? It's a similar case here. First we've to catch our hare.'

CHAPTER 7

Shooting the nitro man had given a welcome boost to Cade Kellerman's mood. Killing did that to him, it had the effect that a stiff drink might have had on a more normal and well-balanced individual. All that was needful now was to murder the men who had been riding with him for so long and then he might be able to find a way of stealing some money before returning home. Then it would be a matter of lying low for a space, until the assumption was made that he had died with his gang. From what he had seen of the effects of nitroglycerin, there would scarcely be any identifiable body left after the nitro man's barn had been detonated. He would be able to vanish.

Kellerman had made up his mind that Jimmy Storm-cloud would have to go with the rest. True, the 'breed was a useful man, but what was really needed was a clean break, with nobody looking for him and not a living soul being aware that he still walked the earth.

It was still early morning when Cade Kellerman rode into Cedar Rapids. He did not head for the Metropole, he'd no intention of spending more than one night in any location, at least while men were still trying to track him down. It would be different after the explosion, when the general consensus would surely be that he and all his men had died while preparing for some villainy or other. Kellerman had already told Jimmy Storm-cloud of his plans, or at least as much of them as was wholesome for the 'breed to know about. There had been no sentimental objections when Kellerman had told him that he proposed to make a clean sweep of all their former comrades. It was, in a way, a pity that Jimmy Storm-cloud would also have to go, but leaving him alive would be too much of a risk. Kellerman glanced up at the clock on the front of the civic hall. It lacked five minutes to nine and he had arranged to meet his conspirator in this business at nine. He quickened his pace.

Jimmy the 'breed was waiting for Kellerman. The young man was staring into the window of a store selling household wares, for all the world as though he were some bona fide shopper, looking to buy a new broom or something. When he caught sight of Kellerman, he gave a jerk of his head, to indicate that the two of them should walk down the street together. As they strolled along the boardwalk, Jimmy Storm-cloud said quietly, 'Morgan's dead.'

'What'd he die of?'

'Shot. Knifed a lawman and the fellow's partner did for him.'

Kellerman grunted noncommittally, which prompted the 'breed to observe, 'Happen you'll not be grieving overmuch over it.'

'Happen not. You can carry word to the others this morning? Tell them that the bank is on and that we've the wherewithal to take it down.'

Jimmy Storm-cloud gave Kellerman a sidelong glance and said, 'Time to lay down. What's your purpose?'

'Lure them out of town and then kill them.' He gave a brief account of the trap that he had laid up at the nitro man's little manufactory. His companion said nothing, which caused Kellerman to ask ironically, 'You ain't turned squeamish, I hope?'

Jimmy Storm-cloud turned a cold eye on the boss and said, 'I ain't squeamish, but if you're planning to serve me the same way as you are the others, I tell you here and now, it'll cost you your life.'

'You always were one for plain speaking. I ain't a fixin' for to kill you. I figure that the two of us could work together and maybe just pick up with one or two others, then and when, as we need them. I had enough o' running a gang. What d'you say, just you and me?'

'Sound fine and good to me. But you recollect, I'm a horse of a different colour from Harker.'

Cade Kellerman laughed at that and clapped the other man on the shoulder in an amicable fashion.

Judas himself, when he was kissing our saviour, could not have played his part better than Kellerman. All that the 'breed said made it more and more likely that here was a man who could not be trusted and would be likely at some future time to be a hindrance and a nuisance. Any doubts that Kellerman had entertained about the wisdom of killing this man along with all the others evaporated like the morning dew in the course of this brief conversation.

After sending the telegram to Pinkertons in Chicago, Ben Walters and young Jackson walked back towards the Metropole. It would be hard to imagine a more ill-matched pair; the grizzled old man, who looked as tough as they come, and the well-dressed boy, who could not have been shaving much more than a year or two. As they passed a narrow street leading off to the left, Abernathy Jackson gave an audible gasp and exclaimed, 'There's the man who booked into the hotel with Cade Kellerman!'

Walters winced at the idea of speaking so loudly of such matters and said softly, 'Keep it down a little and stop staring at him. You sure it's him?'

'I'd take oath on it in a court of law. I saw him just this morning, when the clerk was asking after Kellerman. It's him all right.'

'Well then, let's take a look and see what he's about. Don't stare so, you'll spook him. Here, let's look in this store's window for a moment.'

For Ben Walters, subterfuge and cunning were, in

a sense, second nature. During his years on the scout, he had relied upon the ability to deceive others as to what he planned, but even later, when he had settled down and become respectable, Walters still had not lost that devious streak. No man becomes a great landowner and person of consequence unless he has the skill of being able to mislead others about his intentions when necessary. Taking Jackson's arm, he turned him so that the two of them were gazing into a window that contained a display of agricultural implements whose use were wholly obscure to the young man.

In a low voice, Walters said, 'That fellow's making sure that nobody's on his trail. He's a cautious one all right!'

After looking in the window for a few seconds, Walters indicated that they should continue along the street. The man they were following was by now fifty yards ahead of them and walking at a leisurely amble, from time to time stopping and apparently taking an interest in the displays outside various stores. Then, without warning, he slipped into the space between two buildings. From what Ben Walters had seen of the town's topography, this led to some empty lots that lay behind the First National Bank. Quick as a flash, he grabbed Jackson's arm and pulled him into the nearest store. Without wasting any time, Walters took out his badge and showed it to the fellow behind the counter, saying, 'I'm a peace officer in pursuit of a suspect. Do you have a window opening out on the back of this building?'

'Why yes, through that door to my storeroom. The window there opens out at the back.'

Without wasting any more words, Walters strode through the door thus indicated, with Abernathy Jackson trailing behind him. Walters had taken up position at the edge of the window. He said, 'Just stay where you are. Don't go near the window.'

'What are you doing?'

'I'm watching that fellow and trying to figure out what he's about. It's no coincidence that he's ferreting around at back of the bank, but I can't quite make out what he's doing there.'

There was some excuse for the old man's bewilderment, for the man they had followed seemed to be showing no interest at all in the rear of the bank itself. Instead, he was inspecting various piles of garbage, old lumber and so on that people tend to deposit wherever an empty lot is to be found. He strolled around casually, peering down from time to time to look under some old piece of broken furniture or heap of mouldering paper. He did not so much as glance at the bank building itself. At last, evidently satisfied, he went back the way that he had come, emerging out of the alleyway. Walters and his young companion followed the man, but he simply went back to the Metropole.

Walters and Jackson stood on the sidewalk opposite the hotel, watching the quarry go back to where he was staying. Ben Walters said, 'Well boy, what do you make of it?'

'Well, I guess it has some reference to robbing the bank, but beyond that I wouldn't care to go.'

'What do you reckon they might want with the bank? I mean what do you think they'll be after stealing?'

Jackson thought this question over for a space, before saying slowly, 'Well, I don't think that it'll be silver. The weight of it would be too much.'

Ben Walters' face lit up and, for only the second time since his wife's death, he smiled. He said, 'You've a right shrewd mind, you know that? No, it won't be silver. Mostly likely just cash money, bills and such. But I wouldn't have thought there'd be enough in that bank to satisfy a dozen desperate men. The chief of the money will be locked in their vault, the only cash they'll be like to get will be whatever the clerks at the counter have in their drawers. Say a few hundred or so. That wouldn't go far if shared out between ten or a dozen men. It's a regular conundrum.'

After killing Patrick Carstairs, Kellerman had ridden back to Cedar Rapids and by prior arrangement met the 'breed in a little saloon on the other side of town from the Metropole. There, he reasoned the case out to Jimmy Storm-cloud. 'Killing the others'll be as easy as pie. If I can just get them all near to that shack, I can take out the lot of 'em in one blow.'

'Where does that leave us,' asked the other man,

observing Cade Kellerman's face closely; searching for evasion or falsehood. 'Where's our profit in the transaction?'

'Why, with those others out the way, we simply steal some money and then high-tail out of here. Return to our homes and lay low for a time.'

'It sounds easy, when you say it fast like that,' said Jimmy Storm-cloud. 'What are we aiming for to steal and how does this high-tailing out of town work?'

Kellerman looked at his companion approvingly. In some ways, it was a pity that the 'breed had to die. He was without doubt the sharpest and most ruthless of the current members of the Kellerman Gang. He said, 'You're not still mistrustful of me, I hope? Here's the way of it. We're going to take cash, enough to last us for a month or two, before we line anything else up. We both need to stay out of sight for a few weeks at the least.' He then proceeded to outline to Jimmy Storm-cloud just how they were going to steal cash from the bank and then make a swift getaway, with not the least possibility of anybody being able to pursue them. Before that could be accomplished though, there was one task that the 'breed would need to undertake for their mutual benefit and advantage. Sitting there in a shadowy and secluded corner of the barroom, Kellerman outlined this and received grudging agreement that the other would do it.

*

The rest of Kellerman's boys were growing a little weary of being cooped up in various low lodging houses. There was some little muttering about their boss and the hope was vehemently expressed that he knew what he was doing and that they would soon be flush again with funds. None of them had actually spoken to Kellerman himself since they had arrived in Cedar Rapids, it being thought that since he was the most recognizable of them all, it would set them in hazard were he to be seen in their company. That at least was how Jimmy Storm-cloud represented the case to them when he acted as Cade Kellerman's mouth-piece or emissary. It would, he said, be too dangerous for all of them to meet up here in town. Instead, the boss was sending word that he would meet them a few miles from Cedar Rapids and that he would then make everything plain to them. This meeting was to take place the next day at ten in the morning.

The feeling that they had been wronged or cheated was growing stronger in the breasts of some of the members of his outfit and at least three had determined that they would speak their mind when next they saw Kellerman. Word had spread that the boss himself had been seen coming out of the grandest hotel in town, while they were forced to contend with bedbugs in unsavoury little boarding houses. It was not to be borne much longer and if Kellerman really had planned to meet with his men the next day, then there was every chance that things might have gone ill for him. There was mutiny in the wind.

*

Ben Walters felt a little uneasy about booking into the same hotel as one of the men he was determined to bring to justice, one way or another, but the Metropole was such a pleasant contrast to those nights he had lately spent sleeping out of doors that he couldn't resist staying there. Since arriving in Cedar Rapids, he had visited a barber for a shave and now he was luxuriating in a hot bath, to soak away the grime of his journey. He lay back and considered what he might do over the next few days. As an aid to thought, Walters draped the wet flannel over his eyes to blot out the world and just lay musing.

Meeting that boy had been an amusing piece of fortune. He did not really think that Abernathy Jackson would really be much use in tracking down and tackling Kellerman and his boys, but it was nice to meet a young fellow with such grit. Mentally, he compared Jackson with his own sons and they were found wanting. Neither had that streak of toughness that to Ben Walters was the mark of a real man. They were both of them as soft as their mother. Abernathy Jackson might be from a good family and highly educated, but he had been perfectly prepared to shoot Walters up on that rooftop. He couldn't imagine either of his own boys being so determined about anything. All they cared about was high living. Well, that's how it was sometimes in this world.

There was a sharp rap at the door to Walters'

room. The room containing the bath was off his bedroom and he had left the connecting door open. He cleared his throat and called out, 'Come right in!' There was a pause and then he heard the pleasantly modulated voice of young Jackson, calling interrogatively, 'Hallo, anybody in?'

'I'm here in the bath. Come in, if you ain't too shy.'

'I'm not shy,' said the young man and walked straight into the room, saying, 'Hope I'm not disturbing you, sir?'

'Not a bit of it. I'm thankful to be disturbed, anyway. When I'm alone, I get to thinking too much.'

Although he wasn't in general one for discussing his affairs with anybody, let alone complete strangers, Walters had given Jackson the bare bones of his tale; enough to explain what he had been doing up on that roof and why he was dead set on hunting down the Kellerman Gang. Young Jackson had said nothing, but merely listened and nodded. Now, he said, 'Were I you, I reckon I might not want to brood on what's past either.'

It was exactly the right note to strike and Walters wondered how a youth who had never met him before in his life, until a few hours earlier, could be so delicate about the matter. He said gruffly, 'Reach me that towel and I'll get dressed. You're full young, I suppose you want to be up and doing, rather than waiting patiently. Young folk are always that way.'

It was late afternoon and Abernathy Jackson was

110

indeed anxious to be out and finding what plans the men they were hunting might have. For the older man, there was not so much of a hurry, but Jackson had a ticking clock in his head and ever since they had sent that telegram to Pinkertons he lived in dread of a posse of agents arriving before he had had a chance to prove himself. The sooner that he and his strange companion went into action, the better he would like it.

Jimmy Storm-cloud sat motionless on his horse, surveying the scene below him. The little wooden shack and the old barn looked as though they were both utterly devoid of life, but the 'breed had not succeeded in living to his present age by taking things for granted. He sat there for a full quarter hour, just watching and listening. At last, reasonably satisfied in his own mind that he was not about to ride into an ambush, he squeezed his legs tight and set the horse walking slowly and carefully down the slope.

The 'breed was always wary of treachery and he didn't trust Cade Kellerman a bit. How if Kellerman had indeed murdered the nitro man as he had said, but was now trying to shift the blame for his death onto his supposed confidant? It was the kind of trick that Jimmy Storm-cloud could easily imagine playing himself on somebody he was eager to be rid of. Now that he had come here on the errand that Kellerman had sent him, he thought that he might as well have a look about and see if the evidence supported what he had been told. This was another thing about Jimmy Storm-cloud; he lived his life on the assumption that all those he met were lying to him and most likely wishing to cheat him out of something or other.

After dismounting, the 'breed drew his pistol and, without knocking, kicked open the door of the dwelling. There was nobody inside and the door swung lazily on its leather hinges. He entered the single room and wrinkled his nose. The overpowering, coppery stink told him at once that blood had been shed here, a fair quantity of the stuff. Pulling aside the rough woollen blanket that obscured his view of what might lie under the bed, he bent down and looked. Well, that part at least of Cade Kellerman's story had been true.

There didn't look to be anything worth stealing in the room, presumably the nitro man had a buried stash of money or gold somewhere. Jimmy Storm-cloud poked about a little, but could find no sign of any portable wealth. Having drawn a blank, he left the squalid room and strolled over to the barn. Before he reached it, somebody hailed him from the higher ground about the stream and when he turned it was to see a tough and capable-looking man loping down the slope towards him, his face set in angry lines. When this fellow reached the level ground where the 'breed was standing, he strode up to him and said truculently, 'What were you doing in my brother's house?'

This was a facer and no mistake. Kellerman had not said anything about the man he had murdered having a brother. Jimmy Storm-cloud prevaricated skilfully, saying, 'What house do you mean?'

This seemed to irritate the newcomer, who said, 'Are you making game of me? How many houses d'ye see hereabouts?'

'Oh, you mean yon pig pen? I was looking for the owner, to talk over a little business.' Even as he replied in this way, Jimmy Storm-cloud knew that this was a complication that would need to be dealt with, and that right quick. Preferably before the man went into that shack and found his brother's corpse.

Patrick Carstairs' brother looked something less than enchanted to hear the house being described as a pig pen. For a moment, it looked as though he was about to launch a furious assault upon the man standing in front of him. Then he evidently changed his mind, turning on his heel and walking briskly and purposefully towards the little cabin. Whereupon Jimmy Storm-cloud drew his pistol and shot the man in the back. He fired twice more, just to make sure, and then, to be on the safe side, he went over and fired once more, this time through the head of the man who had fallen to the ground, dying.

As far as he could see, this second corpse would only need to be concealed for twenty-four hours or so. By tomorrow afternoon, he and Kellerman would be away out of Cedar Rapids, with little prospect of anybody being able to follow them. After that it wouldn't matter if this man were to be found. He dragged the dead body unceremoniously into the wooden dwelling house and attempted to shove it under the bed, where the corpse of his brother already had a cloud of flies buzzing around it. There was no room for a second body and so he threw it onto the bed and covered it inadequately with the blankets.

The inside of the barn was just how Kellerman had described it. There were shelves, with rows of bottles and jars on them, retorts, spirit lamps, glass tubing and various tubs. Had he not been previously apprised of the purpose of the place, the 'breed would certainly have taken it to be the still of a moonshiner. In one corner stood serried ranks of brown, earthenware demijohns, the ones that Kellerman said were full of the finished product.

There weren't many things that were likely to make Jimmy Storm-cloud nervous, but this stuff certainly caused him to take a little more care than usual about what he was doing. To trip and fall with one of those things in his hands would very likely mean the end of him. Gingerly, he picked up one of the jars by the two rings jutting out from the neck of the flagon. Then he walked very slowly outside to where his horse stood waiting patiently. Before setting out, he had rigged up a harness of wire and cloth, such as would cradle the flagon upright as he returned to Cedar Rapids.

The slope up from the stream was so gentle that, in the usual way of things, Jimmy Storm-cloud would have cheerfully urged his mount on to a gallop to see if he couldn't reach the top before those riding along of him. With ten pounds' weight of treacherously sensitive explosive stowed at the front of his saddle though, he felt disinclined to take any chances. He accordingly led the horse up to the higher ground, walking beside him at a gentle walking pace. There really was no percentage in taking risks in this matter.

Cold-blooded and cruel he may have been, but Jimmy Storm-cloud was careful enough about preserving his own life. Just as he was about to swing himself up in the saddle, he thought better of it and withdrew his foot from the stirrup. It took him almost two hours to get back to Cedar Rapids, escorting his horse on foot and leading him by the bridle. That way, he could be perfectly sure that he was able to spot any holes in the road, stones or anything else that might have caused the beast to rear up or fall down. Even so, by the time that he got back to town, the 'breed was clammy with sweat. It was with a sense of enormous relief that he was able to carry the demijohn of nitro up to his room at the Metropole.

Even now, he was not easy in his mind. Suppose that the change of temperature from the barn to the hotel room was too great and that the liquid in the jar began to deteriorate? He would be mightily glad when this stage of the game was over.

CHAPTER 8

Although he did not know precisely what was
planned, Ben Walters had a pretty shrewd idea of
how the Kellerman Gang would be taking action in
the next few days. He knew that they would be doing
whatever it was they had in mind within forty-eight
hours or so, because it stood to reason that they
would not be wanting to stay all together in the same
big town much longer. At a guess, after the failure of
the express train robbery, they wouldn't be too flush
financially and would be wanting some quick money.

The First National Bank clearly featured somewhere in the plans, but whether that was on account
of all that silver stored there or because they hoped
just to steal a heap of cash, Walters could not say.
What he was sure of though was their means of
escape. It was just too tempting, the railroad depot
being across the street from the bank. With a prop-
erly organized police force and the ability to call
upon the nearby army base at need, there would be

no sense in staging a robbery and then riding away on horseback. No, the depot must fit into the plans somewhere and Ben Walters was fairly sure that he knew how. On the Friday morning, he rose early and before breakfast took a turn down main street to the depot.

Cedar Rapids was a terminal station for the line running between there and Des Moines. No trains ran through the town, all terminated there. Three lines ran into Cedar Rapids, from Des Moines, Chicago and St Pauls. Those travelling between Chicago and Des Moines were obliged to change trains at Cedar Rapids. Looking around the station, Walters struck up a conversation with a uniformed porter, an old-timer like himself. He said, 'Pardon me for asking, but are all these lines just single tracks? What happens if a train heading from here to Chicago should meet one going in the opposite direction? Wouldn't there be a nasty smash?'

'Well sir, it takes a bit of arranging, but no, in general we don't have all that many accidents.'

Ben Walters was tolerably familiar with the way that railroads ran, but thought that this might be a way of starting a casual chat in order to find out what he really wished to know, which was how long it took to fire up a locomotive and how easy it would be to make off with one, were a body to be that way inclined. The answers to his questions were simple. The engines were fired up and ready to go some quarter hour before they left the depot and taking

118

one without permission would not be difficult, always providing somebody knew how to start the thing.

After he had ended his little chat with the old porter, Walters left the depot, casting an eye over the telegraph wires that ran overhead. He reckoned that a few shots at the porcelain insulators would most likely bring them down and render them unfit for their purpose.

Although he did not realize it, Walters came within a matter of seconds of bumping into the man whose actions had deprived his wife of her life. Less than a minute after he had left the depot, heading back to the Metropole to have breakfast, Cade Kellerman entered from another direction and checked that he had been correct about his earlier estimations of what would be needful if he and Jimmy Storm-cloud were to be able to escape scot-free from Cedar Rapids, vanishing like ghosts.

From all that Kellerman could make out, he would arrive back at his home with perhaps five hundred dollars in bills. There would be no question this time of having to sell gold or silver bullion cheaply, receiving only a fraction of its market value. The money he took that afternoon would be all his with nobody to claim a share. He figured that he could live comfortably for months, without the need to carry out any more jobs. Time enough for everybody in law enforcement to forget all about his face and name.

Cade Kellerman was like a squirrel in that he was

accustomed to picking up little nuggets of information and then storing them away for months or even years until the time came to make best advantage of them. Lesser men might learn something interesting about a bank and then rush off that very day to carry out a robbery against it, but that had never been Kellerman's way. He stockpiled little snippets and then fell back on them during lean times such as this. He had heard better than a year since that the First National Bank obliged some of its bigger customers in Cedar Rapids by sending a messenger to their premises and collecting their week's taking on a Friday afternoon and then bringing it to the bank, thus saving them a little trouble. Only the Metropole hotel, a big store and the largest eating house in the town were favoured in this way.

Of course, while he was riding with a dozen other men, it would hardly be worth fetching his gang all the way here just to snatch four or five hundred dollars. It was a different matter though if the money was to be his alone. As he strolled back to the hotel where he had stayed the previous night, Cade Kellerman congratulated himself upon his cunning and foresight. All that now remained was to rid himself of his one-time comrades in arms and then he would be free to return home and spend a few months planning his next course of action.

Abernathy Jackson was still fretting that the men from the Pinkertons head office in Chicago would arrive before he'd had a chance to stake a proper claim to the Kellerman Gang. Walters reassured him over breakfast, saying, 'I don't look for those Pinkertons' boys to be here earlier than tonight. We'll have dealt with things before then.'

'How so?'

'I'm guessing that those fellows we're after are fixing to carry out a robbery this very day. It has some reference to the bank, but I'm hazy on the precise details.'

'What's to hinder them from staying longer here? Why d'you say that they are going to act today?'

Ben Walters was not in the habit, and had not been so for many years, of having his authority questioned in this way. Mastering an urge to tell this young whippersnapper to mind his manners and do as he was bid, Walters said, 'Waiting 'til Monday would add three days to their stay in town. They won't want to hang around here for that long. The bank will be closed tomorrow and also on the sabbath. They'll have to do what they plan today and I reckon it will be in the late afternoon.'

'I see that. You want that we should stake out the bank and wait for them to move?'

'Nothing o' the sort!' exclaimed Walters, horrified. 'Why, they outnumber us by five or six to one. It'd be a massacre. No, I have something else in mind.'

Sitting there in the eating area of the Metropole hotel, Walters set out his ideas to the young man

Jimmy Storm-cloud had spread word to all the other members of the gang that the boss would meet them out of town at midday. There had been a not inconsiderable amount of grumbling, coupled with remarks about folks who were riding high and thought they were better than the rest of them. The 'breed smirked at this and hoped that this would infuriate the men to whom he was talking even more. He wanted them to arrive at the rendezvous good and mad, with their grievances bubbling away within them. That way, they would be more likely to be angry and careless. This would in turn mean that they would be less apt to notice anything amiss, so eager would they be to meet up with their leader and express their views. It was plain that they had been talking the matter over and were ready to present a united front to Kellerman.

Cade Kellerman had shared his plans fully with Jimmy Storm-cloud, and as a consequence it was in his interests too that everybody showed up at the nitro man's shack. For this reason, he took no steps to placate the anger of some of those he went to visit. It was vital that they were all near that barn at midday today. He himself was hoping to slip out of town without being marked, so that he could ride his horse a few miles, leading that belonging to Kellerman as he went. Six or seven miles should do the trick.

*

Although he had been in a way relieved to team up with the old man, Abernathy Jackson was still a mite ticked off that his scheme for glory had in some obscure way been commandeered by Ben Walters. Although he had not really known how to proceed, having found his man, he still felt that he deserved a say in how matters progressed. He intimated as much to Walters that Friday morning, as they walked down to the railroad depot. He said, 'You know sir, that if not for me you wouldn't even know for sure that Kellerman was in town?'

'I'll allow that, son,' replied Walters. 'But then again, if not for me, you'd still be running around aimlessly, with no idea how to go about things.'

Jackson reddened at this and said sharply, 'I mean to have a hand in bringing him to justice, you know. You needn't think that you're going to run this show all by yourself.'

In point of fact, this was just exactly what Ben Walters had been thinking. He had planned to send the youngster off on some fool's errand and take care of Cade Kellerman single-handedly, man to man. Something of this must have shown in his face, because Jackson exclaimed, 'My God, you were, weren't you? Well you needn't think it for a moment. I'll take him down myself, rather.'

'Hold up,' said Walters, horrified at the idea of the young man tackling the job alone. 'First off is where

Cade Kellerman would make short work of you. Secondly, we'll work as a team. I promise that we won't leave each other's side and that whatever happens, we'll be equal partners. Is that a deal?'

Jackson looked searchingly into the other man's face and saw only sincerity there. He said, 'You give me your oath on it?'

'I do. For good or ill, we'll see this through together.'

It was a damned nuisance, thought Walters, but there it was. The boy had a fair point. He'd just have to try and make sure that no harm befell the fellow, who was far too decent to be mixed up in this sort of game. Aloud, he said, 'We need to know just exactly when trains are coming in and going out of the depot. I don't want that we should end up causing a train wreck ourselves, that would be a terrible thing.'

'You think that we'll be able to pull this off?'

'We won't know until we try. But I'm hopeful of success. You know that we're like to be dealing with a dozen armed men, though.'

'You don't seem at all worried about it all.'

'Any man,' said Ben Walters, 'Who says as he ain't afeared of death in such circumstances is either a mad fool or a liar. And you don't strike me as the former. Make sure that you stay a little scared and that will stop you getting careless.'

As Walters had outlined the plan to his young companion, the only way that those boys could raise money and then get out of town without pursuit would be to steal some ordinary cash money, bills, and then take a locomotive and tender down the line. They would be sure to take out the telegraph line leading that way as well, if he knew anything about such things. Finding their trail after that would be next door to impossible.

Of course, Ben Walters had no idea that Kellerman was aiming to rid himself of the greater part of his gang before undertaking his escape, but other than that, Walters' reading of the situation was spot on. That being so, it remained only to figure out the times in which a locomotive would be fired up and ready to go and not at hazard of smashing head-long into a train approaching from the opposite direction.

The other nine members of the Kellerman Gang, apart from Jimmy Storm-cloud and Cade Kellerman himself, drifted out of Cedar Rapids inconspicuously, in ones and twos, on the morning of Friday, July 18th 1873. Most were feeling a little vexed with their leader and prepared for some plain talking. The directions that the 'breed had given them were very clear and explicit. He was keen to ensure that nobody took a wrong turning and that all the nine men were present in the vicinity of the nitro man's business premises at noon that day. It would raise all manner of complications should even one of those boys miss the appointment and end up wandering around aimlessly, apt to fall prey to the law. There was no telling what a body might say under such circumstances, if he felt he was in danger of hanging. It was vital that all nine of them should die that day.

Two of the nine rode together out of Cedar Rapids. Joe Williams and Ezra Dixon had known each other for years, before they had ever joined up with Cade Kellerman and the rest. They had done well by riding with Kellerman, but both now thought that it was time to move on and perhaps work by themselves for a spell. Even so, they had resolved to hear what Kellerman had to say on the off chance that it might profit them.

'I weren't sorry to hear 'bout Harker,' said Ezra Dixon. 'He was a right contentious son of a bitch and I was minded to kill him myself before now.'

'Yes, it was funny to hear him squealing when Kellerman held him in the fire,' said Williams, smiling at the memory. 'He won't be missed.'

'I don't trust the 'breed. He's riding high, but there's something more.'

His friend turned and looked hard at Dixon and said, 'I mind the same thing. He always was a cocksure cow's son, but he's gloating over something now, mark what I say.'

Without speaking further, the two men reined in and looked at each other. At length, Joe Williams said quietly, 'You smell treachery in this?'

Dixon rubbed his chin thoughtfully, saying, 'Maybe. Let's you and me keep an eye out for anything tending in that way.' Then he urged on his horse.

There was no difficulty in finding the place described by Jimmy Storm-cloud. There was nothing else of note thereabouts. Dixon and Williams tied their mounts up at a sapling on the ridge above the little stream and looked down at the scene below. Six men were milling around aimlessly, smoking and chatting. Their horses were also secured on the high ground above them. Despite their misgivings, neither Joe Williams nor Ezra Dixon could see how the 'breed or Kellerman could play them false if they went down the slope to join the others. There were, when all was said and done, eight of them and even if Jimmy Storm-cloud started shooting at them from under cover, they would scatter and then catch up with him. It could do no possible harm to at least go and see the others.

For the last two hours, Cade Kellerman had been lying prone on the high ground across the stream from the nitro man's dwelling house and place of work. He was just inside a spinney of pine trees and had, when he laid down, made sure to cover himself with branches and leaf litter so that anybody looking in his direction from down below would see nothing likely to make them suspicious. Even with a pair of field glasses trained straight on the spinney, nothing would be seen. Only the very end of Kellerman's rifle's muzzle was poking out of the leaves and twigs, and it was pointing unwaveringly at the two gallons of nitroglycerin that he had placed at the rear of the barn by the stream.

127

The others greeted Dixon and Williams soberly. There were no high jinks and the atmosphere of all those present was thoughtful and sombre. Dixon consulted his pocket watch and said, 'By my reckoning, it lacks but a minute or two 'til noon. Who's missing?'

'Kellerman and the 'breed, for two,' said somebody, which caused a chuckle. It turned out that only Brent Casey was missing, apart from the other two men. Dixon had a superb sense of danger and his antennae were twitching now, for no obvious reason. He looked around the little clearing, but there was nothing to be seen that might have caused any uneasiness.

Joe Williams was also feeling apprehensive. He said, 'Anybody looked in that cabin or barn?' It appeared that nobody had yet done so. Some sixth sense was at work, impelling both Williams and Dixon to be fearful of an ambush. The two of them strolled over to the barn and pulled open the door. There was nobody inside and at first the two of them both guessed that this was some moonshiner's lair. The smell was strange though, not a bit like distilled alcohol. They could neither of them think what other purpose might be served by all those flasks and tubes.

'What about the house?' asked Williams, 'Think we might have look there, too?'

Ezra Dixon looked around the barn again. He was sure that he was missing some vital clue that might shed light upon the current situation. He said, 'Take out your pistol and we'll act like somebody might be hid in there. Something's not right. You feel it too?'

Williams did indeed feel that something was amiss. The hairs on the nape of his neck were prickling and there was a heaviness in the air, such as one gets before a storm. He and Dixon drew their pistols and walked over to the shack. The others watched them, wondering what the play was. When they reached the door, the two men positioned themselves one either side of it. Then Williams moved round very fast, kicked the door open and immediately moved back to one side. There was no sudden burst of gunfire from within though. He and Dixon looked at each other and nodded slightly to each other. Then they both rushed in, one after the other.

Their aim might have been to overpower by main force anybody who was waiting for them within the squalid little building, but Williams and Dixon soon discovered that they didn't need to worry about that. It was plain as could be that nobody was laying low, hoping to surprise them when they entered. This did nothing though to allay their fears, because the stench of blood and death was overwhelming within the hut. It struck both men that murder had probably been done here and the obvious question next to ask was by whom and for what purpose?

The pounded clay floor was besmeared with dried blood and the rank smell of it hung in the air. Even stronger was the stench of decay. Joe Williams exclaimed, 'Christ, what a stink!' He and his friend cast their eyes around the place and soon spotted that the bed appeared to be occupied. Neither of them was squeamish, but both hesitated to pull off the blankets and see what lay under them. Eventually, Dixon did so and revealed the body of a man who had been shot several times in the back and once through the head. Pulling the bedclothes around in that way had disturbed a cloud of flies, who had been feasting on something. The focus of their attention seemed to be not the corpse on the bed, but rather something underneath. Ezra Dixon bent down and saw that there was a second dead body secreted there.

Although neither of them could say just what they suspected, there was something about all this that made them think that hanging around in the vicinity was not likely to be healthful. They left the cabin and, once in the open air, Williams called to the other men, who were standing around, keen to know what was going on, 'There's something amiss. We'd best not linger here.'

Up on the slope, where he waiting to kill his erst-while comrades in arms, Cade Kellerman muttered an oath. He could see that in another second there would be a general panic flight and all the others would flee from the spot. If only Brent Casey would appear. He dared not fire until he was sure of taking them all at one go. Then he caught a glimpse of movement on the ridge opposite and saw that Casey had arrived and was leading his horse to a tree. With maddening slowness, he looped the reins around a branch and then began walking down the slope. Down below, one of the men shouted to Casey, 'Get back. It's a trap.' Another second and there would be a general flight. Just then, the sun passed behind a cloud, casting a sudden gloom upon the scene below. Kellerman just hoped that the blast would be enough to take out Brent Casey as well at the distance he was from the barn. He carefully sighted down the barrel and squeezed the trigger.

There was a blinding white light, which lit up the area as though lightning had flashed. At once, Kellerman dropped his face into the leaf mould. He'd no wish to be struck in the face by any flying debris. A fraction of a second after the flash of light came a shaking of the ground and then, hot on the heels of that, came the noise; a crashing roar, like a clap of thunder. Still, Cade Kellerman lay face down in the dirt. A hail of stones, twigs, clods of earth and pieces of wood began to rain down on his back. Only when it had altogether ceased did he look up.

The clearing had been scythed clean of life. The barn and cabin were no longer there and the trees that fringed the stream were as bare as though it was mid-winter. All their leaves had been stripped off by the blast. Kellerman could see Casey lying motionless on the sloping ground. It looked as though his fears of the explosion not being powerful enough to account for him as well had been unfounded.

The mare was whinnying in fear and distress. She must have thought that the end of the world had come, thought Kellerman. Confident that he was not in any danger now from his former friends, he shook off his covering and went into the trees to comfort the frightened beast. There was a savage joy in his breast, for he knew now that it was only necessary to kill one more man and he would then be free of the toils that he had lately felt were about to crush him to death.

After mounting up, Kellerman cast his eyes once more over the scene of devastation that lay below him. He muttered under his breath, 'Well, so long boys! I'm sorry it had to end this way, but I thought it was for the best.' Then he dug his knees into the mare's flanks and rode off towards Cedar Rapids.

CHAPTER 9

While Cade Kellerman was murdering nine men, Abernathy Jackson was riding out with Walters, following the railroad line that connected Cedar Rapids with Des Moines. A dusty track ran alongside the tracks for several miles, before veering off to the north. Although he hadn't shared all his ideas with the younger man, Jackson could tell that Ben Walters had a very clear notion of what he was about. Attempting to reassert his own interest in the matter, he said to Walters, 'You don't think that the Pinkertons men are likely to arrive 'til late tonight?'

'If they do, it's not going to be until nightfall or thereabouts. It'll all be over by then.'

'Meaning?'

'Meaning that Cade Kellerman and his boys will either be dead or under lock and key. Or, of course, we'll be dead. But in such a case, the least of your worries will be what happens when the Pinkertons arrive on the scene.'

'And you promise that I'll get. . . .'

'Yes, yes,' said Walters impatiently. 'If we kill or capture them, then I'll ensure that the deed redounds to your credit and not mine. That satisfy you?'

'I didn't mean . . .'

'You talk a lot, you know that?'

The land in those parts was mainly flat, apart from some wooded slopes rising to the left of the track that they were presently following. Walters seemed to be searching for something, although what it might be Abernathy Jackson had no idea. They had been trotting along the track for the better part of two hours and were now some nine or ten miles from town. Then Walters halted and said, 'That's the very place!'

A few hundred yards ahead of them, a spur ran off from the railroad towards the trees. On this length of track stood a single flatbed wagon, of the kind used for carrying logs. In fact, this was just precisely what this wagon had been used for in the past. There had for a while been a logging camp here, which was devoted to felling trees and then hauling them to Cedar Rapids for building purposes. It had gone bust just after the war though and now there stood on the track just this one, single wagon.

When they reached the spot where a set of points joined the spur to the main line, Ben Walters reined in and dismounted. He went over to the points and examined them carefully, grunting with evident satisfaction at what he saw. Then he said sharply, 'Well now, get down from that horse of yours. There's work to be done and I don't aim to undertake it alone.'

Jackson climbed down gingerly from the horse that he had hired that morning. He was not a regular nor enthusiastic rider and he felt pretty sore and uncomfortable. Once down on firm ground, he said, 'What work? I don't rightly understand you.'

By now, Walters had jumped down from his own horse and was examining the abandoned railroad wagon. He said, 'Instead o' talking, whyn't you come over here and lend a hand?'

'What is your purpose?'

'Why, I want to make sure that the two of us can move this wagon along here by brute force.'

The two of them put their shoulders to the rear of the wagon, but nothing happened. Ben Walters said, 'Push, man. I'm forty years older than you and yet I've twice the strength. Push harder.'

Stung by the implication that he was a weakling, Jackson put his whole strength into the business and, slowly, the flatbed started moving along the track towards the mail line. Walters said, 'Whoa, now. Stop. I don't want this here to end up blocking that line. Least not yet awhiles.'

'Not yet? Don't tell me you mean to cause a train to crash into it at some future time?'

'Not a whole, entire train, no. Just a locomotive and tender is what I suspect. Come on, we need to get back to town.'

As they rode back, Walters condescended to

explain what he had in mind. He said, 'Those rascals are going to steal from the bank and then leave town by stealing a locomotive. If I'm right, that is. It's surely what I'd do if I . . . well, if I was a robber. They'll have horses waiting somewhere and nobody'll know where they jumped train. They'll as good as vanish from the face of the earth.'

'You mean to block their way with that wagon? What then?'

'That's up to them. They can throw down their weapons and I'll take them all back to Cedar Rapids.'

'You think they'll surrender to you?'

'No,' said Ben Walters casually, 'I don't think it for a moment.'

Before Jackson could think of a suitable answer to what was in effect a declaration that the man at his side intended to kill a dozen men, Walters said softly, 'Hallo, what have we here?'

Coming along the track towards them at a gentle trot was a man on horseback, leading another mount at his side. As he drew closer, they could see that this was the half-breed that they had followed together; the very same person who had booked into the Metropole with Cade Kellerman. They continued on their way without speaking further, until they were within hailing distance of the fellow, whereupon Walters cried in a cheery voice, 'A very good day to you, stranger.' The other rider grunted something that might have been a greeting or might equally well have been an oath. He carried on his way without even slowing down. Jackson and Walters gave him the road, so that he and his spare mount could pass.

Once the 'breed had passed them, Walters said quietly, 'Don't you look round at him, son. I don't want him spooked none.' The two of them just carried on down the track and Walters turned and fiddled with something at the back of his saddle, glancing backwards as he did so. He announced with satisfaction, 'Well, I don't think he even recognized you. This is a turn-up for the book and no mistake. Unless I'm greatly mistook, we're in for a piece of luck here.'

'How so?'

'Why, have you not been paying heed to what I've told you? Yon fellow is tethering those beasts up somewhere ahead and then he'll be making his way back into town on foot.'

'What then? I don't understand.'

'Why, you pudding head, he's only got two mounts. When him and Kellerman rob the bank, they're going to steal a locomotive and bring it up here. Then they aim to halt it and then, when they're off, to set it going down the line towards Des Moines. Only two horses means that the whole gang isn't here after all, or so I read it. Either that or he's done away with them. Either way, we'll only have the two of 'em to deal with!'

The explosion at the nitro man's abode was very clearly audible in town. Those who knew of the illicit activity being conducted just outside Cedar Rapids shook their heads knowingly. They guessed that some terrible accident had befallen the man. Others assumed that it was a clap of thunder from some distant storm. Jimmy Storm-cloud heard it as he was taking the horses up the line and smiled grimly. He knew that Kellerman was not a man to make any error in the matter of murder and that it was now just him and the boss together in this.

Walters and Jackson got back to Cedar Rapids at about ten minutes to two. The older man seemed sure that they could afford the time to eat and also visit a gunsmith. He had it in mind to acquire a hunting rifle, he said. 'Then again, you need a proper firearm, too,' he observed to Jackson, 'That nickel-plated two-two might serve well enough in a lady's reticule, but it ain't what you'll want if there's any hot action.'

After acquiring what Ben Walters thought they would be needing in the way of weaponry, the two men stopped off at an eating house and filled up on steaks, followed by pancakes and syrup. They sat in a quiet corner of the place, such that they could hold a conversation without the chance of anybody eavesdropping upon them. Walters said, 'Kellerman and his partner will be reaching that place where we fooled around with that wagon at pretty much exactly four-fifty.'

'How can you be so precise? I don't understand.'

'It's not too hard to figure out. Train comes in

from St Pauls at five and twenty to five. Then one leaves from the depot for Des Moines at a quarter to the hour. The bank closes at five and so they'll have to conduct their business before that hour and make a pretty sharp getaway at once. Leave at ten to five and you won't have a locomotive fired up and ready to go. They'll take the thing at twenty minutes to the hour and be at our little ambush in ten minutes or so.'

Set out in that way, this all sounded quite convincing to Abernathy Jackson. There was only one thing that he couldn't quite fathom out. He said, 'I see that you're right about this. Fact that man was taking two horses up that way tells me that. But how could you have guessed that would be their plan? That's what I don't see. I never in a million years would have thought of stealing an engine from the depot like that, yet it was the first thing that occurred to you! How come?'

Walters shrugged. 'Guess I've just that kind of mind. Anyway, this is nothing to the purpose. We need to be getting back, so's to set things up. How's your rear end doing with all this riding? A mite sore, perhaps?'

Abernathy Jackson grinned boyishly. 'Just a little. You think if there's only the two of them, that they might give up without a fight and let us take them back to Cedar Rapids? I'd sure like to have them in custody by the time that the men from Pinkertons show up.'

'Would you go back tamely, knowing that you would hang for sure?'

It was a long and weary walk back to town for Jimmy Storm-cloud. Still, he never minded a little exercise. It was the next stage of the scheme that he was dreading, although he would sooner have died than admit this, even to Cade Kellerman. Especially to Kellerman. He had slept the previous night with a gallon of nitroglycerin in one corner of the room. It had been a humid and sultry night and the 'breed was terrified that the change in weather might be sufficient to set off the nitro, or at the very least cause it to degrade and become unstable. For aught he knew to the contrary, this might indeed have happened.

The matter of the demijohn of nitro was playing on Jimmy Storm-cloud's mind during his walk back to Cedar Rapids because it was an integral part of the plans that he and Kellerman had laid. This would entail him carrying the gallon of explosives to the back of the First National Bank and then detonating it by a rifle shot. He could only guess at the devastation that ten pounds' weight of nitroglycerin would wreak. Certainly, it would be likely to blow down the rear wall of the bank and probably kill those inside. This was not the object though. The explosion would serve to concentrate the attention of everybody in town on the First National Bank and create the impression that it was being robbed. There wouldn't be a soul in town who would be considering that at that very moment, he and the boss would be making off with a locomotive from the depot across the road!

All the pieces of the puzzle were now falling perfectly into place, from all that Cade Kellerman was able to collect. At half past four on the button, the 'breed would set off the diversion by blowing up the bank. Everybody would rush to this spot and all those guards would be readying themselves to defend the silver bullion. Poor, deluded bastards! As soon as the mine was sprung, he would seize the bank messenger and snatch the bag from him. Then he and Jimmy Storm-cloud would uncouple the locomotive and tender from the express to Des Moines and make off with it. There would hardly be anybody watching the train, what with all the fuss and chaos that must inevitably follow the explosion at the First National.

The bank closed promptly at five on Friday afternoons. That meant that the messenger would have to be there at about a quarter to the hour if the cash he brought back was to be counted before closing time. On the other hand, he wouldn't wish to collect the weekly takings from the Metropole and the other two establishments too early in the afternoon. The whole point of banking the money on a Friday like that was so that there wouldn't be too much cash lying around over Saturday and Sunday. Kellerman guessed that the money would be collected at about a quarter after four and delivered to the bank within thirty minutes or so.

At a little after four o'clock that Friday afternoon, two riders reined in and dismounted at the site of the old logging camp alongside the railroad line. As they walked over to the flatbed wagon, the younger of the two asked, 'How will we operate the points to get the wagon on the main line?'

'Won't have to,' said Ben Walters complacently, 'It's held by a spring. It'll let the wagon from this spur pass and then spring back again.' Seeing the puzzled look on the other man's face, Walters continued, 'See, if you could just switch that point there, then sooner or later some fool would leave it switched in the direction of this line and some express train bound out of Cedar Rapids would thunder up the tracks, be diverted onto this spur and then crash into the trees. So there's a leaf spring, which keeps the point closed against this part of the track. You can only get onto this spur from the main line if somebody operates a long boom, like a key, to hold the spring back. Soon as they let go, the thing closes again. Get the idea?'

'Not really,' admitted Jackson frankly. 'But you mean that we can push that wagon onto the main line without doing anything about the point?'

'Sure, it'll open from this side as soon as the wheel flanges push against the leaf spring.'

Walters might have been speaking Chinese to the

young man for all the sense that he could make of it. The important point seemed to be that they would be able to block the track against a locomotive coming down the line.

'All we need to do now is wait for the St Pauls train,' said Walters, 'I surely hope it ain't delayed none. If the driver sees us fooling around here and pushing something on the track, then he'll be sure to raise the alarm as soon as he gets to Cedar Rapids. That ain't what's needed at all.' He pointed at one of the telegraph poles further down the tracks and said drily, 'You'll observe, by the by, that they've taken care that nobody'll be wiring on ahead to ask about their whereabouts.'

Jackson looked where the other indicated and saw that the porcelain insulators were shattered and the telegraph wires trailing on the ground.

While Ben Walters and Abernathy Jackson were gazing anxiously at the distant horizon, hoping to see the telltale smudge of grey smoke that would signal the advent of the railroad train, Cade Kellerman and Jimmy Storm-cloud were setting in motion acts that would ultimately lead to the death of more than a dozen men and women.

Although he had hooked two fingers through the ring-shaped protrusions at the neck of the heavy, earthenware flask, Jimmy Storm-cloud was terrified of dropping the thing or perhaps tripping and sending the gallon of explosive crashing to the ground. His fear had made his hands slippery with sweat and this also provoked another worry; that he would lose his grip on the demijohn because it would slip though his fingers. He was greatly relieved when he reached the space between two buildings that led to the empty lot at the back of the First National Bank.

Somebody had dumped a heap of old lumber near to the back of the bank; an old ottoman, mattress and so on. With infinite care, the 'breed set down the flask near this, concealed a little from view and then walked briskly back to the hotel to fetch his rifle. The sight of men carrying firearms openly was not an unusual one at that time and, although weapons were mostly limited to pistols, there were those with muskets slung casually from their shoulders. Mostly, such men had been, or were going to go, hunting.

The church clock on Main Street said that it was nearly half past four. The timing was perfect. Just as he was walking back into the alleyway, Jimmy Storm-cloud heard the far off, mournful wail of a locomotive. This brought a smile to his lips. The train from St Pauls was bang on time. Things were going just exactly as planned, which was not always the case in affairs of this kind. He unslung the rifle and then slipped a cartridge into the breach. A minute more and it would be time.

Things may have been going smoothly for the man charged with detonating the explosion at back of the

144

bank, but the same could not be said for the other member of the party involved in the robbery. Kellerman's plan had been that as soon as he heard the nitro blow and people began running to investigate, he would simply snatch the bag from the bank messenger and push him to the ground. By the time the man had recovered, Kellerman would be off. It would be no manner of use the fellow raising a hue and cry either; folk would be a sight more concerned with finding out what the hell had caused an explosion like an artillery shell, right slap-bang in the middle of their town.

The only thing was, the bank messenger wasn't only carrying the bag; it was chained to his goddamned wrist. Kellerman had seen this kind of precaution before, it prevented anybody from snatching the thing and also stopped the messenger setting it down somewhere and forgetting about it. Well, it was a damned nuisance, but there it was. If it came to it, he'd just have to do whatever was needful. They would be leaving town for good and being wanted for so many deaths, one more wouldn't affect things overmuch. After all, he would hang if he was caught, regardless of what crime he might commit here. A man could only hang once.

Kellerman was standing across the road from the Metropole, the last stop for the skinny little bank messenger. As he came out of the swinging doors, there was a shuddering roar, like a clap of thunder. Those in the street looked around fearfully and then a pall of smoke began to rise above the First National Bank. It didn't take long for cries of, 'They're robbing the bank!' to begin. Cade Kellerman strode across the street until he was only a couple of feet behind the man carrying the black leather portmanteau.

As soon as the St Pauls train had passed out of sight, heading towards Cedar Rapids, Walters said to his young companion, 'We best move this wagon now. Come.'

Now that it had come to the point, Abernathy Jackson felt a marked reluctance to engage in the blocking of a railroad line. Suppose that Walters was wrong and they succeeded only in derailing the Des Moines express? Some of this hesitation must have shown on his countenance, for the other man said, 'Come, this is where the knife meets the bone. You want in on the game or not? I thought you wanted to be a lawman? This is how it's done.'

Jackson walked slowly to the wagon and set his shoulder behind it. Together, the two of them exerted their full strength, until the wheels began to turn and the wagon edged towards the main line. They pushed harder and the wagon picked up a little speed. There was still a good twenty feet to go though. With both men sweating and grunting, the wheels continued to turn, moving them inexorably towards the track connecting Cedar Rapids with Des Moines.

146

'Just a shade faster,' muttered Walters, his face red with the effort, 'We need to make sure that this thing pushes back that spring and gets past the points. Jackson made one last, superhuman effort and was gratified to feel the wagon's speed increase. Then they were nearly at the points. There was a monetary pause when the wheels struck the rail there, but Ben Walters had been perfectly correct in his estimation of the situation and the momentum carried the wagon on, passing the points with a harsh, metallic clatter. Walters said, 'Stop now! We don't want it going all the way.'

It was a blessed relief to stop pushing and they both rested for a space, without saying anything. When he examined the state of affairs, it was clear to Jackson that any locomotive coming down the tracks from Cedar Rapids would be obliged to stop or otherwise to face the very real possibility of being derailed. One set of wheels had passed the points and were on the main track, while the other wheels were still on the spur. The wagon straddled the line in the most satisfactory fashion.

'We need to get under cover now,' said Walters, 'I reckon we've only fifteen minutes at most before things get hot.' The two of them took up positions behind trees, perhaps fifty yards from where the wagon blocked the line. Ben Walters sighted down the barrel of the hunting rifle he had recently purchased and fiddled a little with the sights. He obviously wanted to be sure that he wasn't going to

147

have any difficulties when things began. He said to Jackson, 'I'm going to send off one shot now, just to be sure I have the range right.'

After the echoes of the single rifle shot had died down, Jackson said, 'You aren't fixing to shoot those men down from ambush, I hope. You are going to call on them first to surrender?'

'Oh, certainly, certainly. Don't make yourself uneasy on that count.'

For all that he had assured Abernathy Jackson that Pinkertons would be unable to get anybody to Cedar Rapids before later that night, Walters was out of his reckoning by eight hours or so. Because of their close association with guarding railroads against attack and tracking down those who robbed trains, the railroad companies gave Pinkertons every facility, up to and including allowing them to run their own private trains along their lines.

As soon as word reached head office in Chicago that the Kellerman Gang were in Cedar Rapids, a squad of men had been assembled and despatched in double-quick time. Alan Pinkerton recognized the name of Abernathy Jackson and assumed that the boy had good reason for sending this telegram. Pinkertons certainly could not pass up the chance, if Kellerman really were in Cedar Rapids. Fortunately, there was a direct line between Chicago and Cedar Rapids. For this reason, the train-load of Pinkertons men were able to ride straight into Cedar Rapids, arriving just after a quarter to five on the day that Cade Kellerman hoped to make his escape and throw any pursuers off his trail.

CHAPTER 10

Dave Hopkins had taken the job of bank messenger because he liked being out and about and not stuck behind a desk all day. It gave him the chance to meet folk as well. In the eighteen months he had had the job, he'd not encountered so much as a speck of trouble. When the explosion happened, Hopkins was shocked and amazed, just like every other citizen of Cedar Rapids. He was about to follow the others in running down Main Street to the bank, to see what had happened, when he felt his arm gripped and he was violently hustled into a space between two buildings. Then somebody attempted to wrench his bag from him. When it didn't come free of the steel handcuff that linked it to his wrist, the man who had pulled him into the alleyway grabbed hold of the bag and began trying to force it open.

'You won't be able to get inside it, you know,' said Dave Hopkins smugly, 'The frame is steel.' He assumed that this was just some random thief, out for a few bucks.

Cade Kellerman wasted no more effort on trying to open the black portmanteau. Instead, he produced a razor-sharp knife, which he plunged into the bank messenger's heart. Then, before the man's heart had even stopped beating, Kellerman let drop the bag and, as soon as it fell to the ground, stamped furiously on the wrist to which it was chained, shattering the bones there. Then he bent down and sliced around the flesh of the wrist, removing the hand entirely. The bag was now free and Kellerman picked it up and walked briskly out of the alleyway and towards the depot. He was careful to keep the chain and steel cuff out of sight as far as possible.

After setting off the nitro, Jimmy Storm-cloud slung the rifle over his shoulder again and walked casually back into the street. When others began to run towards the bank, he also did so. In that way, he attracted no attention and was able to reach first the front of the First National Bank and then to cross the road and enter the depot. Most people were leaving the depot to see what was going on at the bank. The 'breed noted with relief that the St Pauls train had arrived and that the one for Des Moines was seemingly ready and waiting to go. He walked along the train towards the locomotive, hoping that the boss would get there soon. Then somebody gripped his elbow and a gruff voice said, 'You wasn't thinking of leaving alone, I'm hoping?'

'I was afeared things had miscarried,' said Jimmy

Storm-cloud, 'You have the money? Listen, can you drive a locomotive?'

'I can stop and start one. That'll be about enough for us.'

When the two of them reached the cab of the locomotive, it was to find two men there; the engine driver and the stoker. With no ceremony whatsoever, Kellerman pulled his pistol and said, 'You men value your lives, you'd best jump down right now. Don't raise the alarm though, or me and my partner here'll kill the pair of you.' To emphasize the point, the 'breed unslung the musket from his shoulder and pointed it in their direction. It appeared that neither of the men wished to die, because they climbed down quietly and went off without making any sort of fuss. Kellerman said to Jimmy Storm-cloud, 'Lend me a hand here to uncouple the tender from the lead carriage.' This proved to be harder than it looked, entailing one man pulling a handle in the cab of the locomotive and the other heaving away at the coupling from outside. However, when it had been accomplished, the locomotive and its tender of coal were free to move.

Further down the train, in the direction of the booking office, there seemed to be some species of commotion developing, most likely caused by the driver and stoker having revealed that they had been dispossessed of their places by armed men. Jimmy Storm-cloud said, 'Now would be a good time to get moving.'

Kellerman did not deign to reply to this, but grasped first at one brass handle and then spun a wheel. There was a hissing of steam and, with a sharp jolt, the locomotive began to pull out of the depot, heading north. Even the usually taciturn 'breed could not restrain a yell of delight, crying, 'Hooo, we done it! We really done it.'

As they moved along the track at a rapidly increasing speed, the two men gave scarcely a glance at a train coming along the tracks running parallel to their own. It consisted of just two carriages and if Cade Kellerman had not been so overwhelmingly relieved at getting free of Cedar Rapids and nobody being able to pursue him, he might have recollected those railroad timetables that he had scrutinized with such care and wondered why a train from Chicago was heading into the depot now and not much later that night.

Waiting behind the trees at the site of their ambush, Ben Walters and Abernathy Jackson had observed the little train with just two carriages heading towards Cedar Rapids. It passed some distance from the line in which they were interested, not closing in on the northbound line until a mile or so from the depot. A minute after it had passed, Walters said, 'Can you feel the vibrations? Locomotive's heading this way.' He cocked his piece and squinted along the barrel, which was trained on a spot twenty yards ahead of the wagon that had been manhandled across the tracks. Jackson shot him a sharp glance, wondering if the older man was intending just to kill those who arrived at the spot without offering them any chance to put up their hands.

Just when he had assumed that they were home and dry, and his only remaining anxiety would soon be alleviated by putting a bullet in Jimmy Storm-cloud's back, Kellerman came up against an unlooked for obstacle; one that threatened to throw all his carefully laid plans into disarray. The first that his companion knew of the matter was when Cade Kellerman uttered a fearful oath and applied the brakes. As they began to perceptibly slow down, the 'breed exclaimed angrily, 'What the hell are you doing? The horses are a mile on from here.'

'Look for your own self,' said Kellerman grimly. 'We ain't travelling a mile down this track.'

The two men peered ahead and realized that they were not yet out of the woods by any means. Jimmy Storm-cloud made his rifle ready and started scanning the trees that fringed the track alongside the railroad. If anybody was waiting for them, then they would surely be concealed thereabouts. Both he and Kellerman knew that time was vital now and that already their plan had miscarried. The idea had been to send the locomotive speeding onwards towards Des Moines, thus ensuring that nobody knew where they might have left it. As things stood, it would be obvious to anybody minded to follow them from Cedar Rapids that they could not be far away. The shadow of the noose fell across them both once more.

The Pinkertons men arrived at the depot in Cedar Rapids to find the place boiling over like a disturbed ants' nest. Everywhere they looked, people were running around like headless chickens and it took some little while to establish that there had been an explosion at the chief bank in town, with many folk killed, and that this was popularly supposed to be connected with an attempt to rob the same. Then there was the astounding news that a railroad loco-motive had been stolen, just minutes before their own train drew in. There had been those at head office in Chicago who thought that this was no more than a snipe hunt, perhaps a false trail laid by the Kellerman Gang themselves. But now it was plain that the men they hunted were within striking dis-tance. The Pinkertons men checked their weapons, while their leader made arrangements to have the carriages of the Des Moines train, which certainly wouldn't be travelling on to that city this day, shunted onto a siding so that their own train could be moved onto the other line and they could set off in pursuit of the most wanted man in the country.

Once the locomotive had come to a halt at the improvised barrier, Walters called out in a stentorian voice, 'Throw down your guns and you won't be harmed.'

Sheltering in the cab, out of sight of Walters and

Jackson, Cade Kellerman shouted back, 'Whoever you be, you bit of more'n you can chew. Leave us be and we'll let you alone.'

Returning no answer, Ben Walters let fly a single shot, which flew unerringly to the footplate of the locomotive's cab and ricocheted up, nearly hitting Kellerman. The men behind the trees had one great advantage over those in the cab, which was their targets were clearly in view. For Kellerman and the 'breed though, there were dozens of trees behind which men might be hiding. And all the while, time was passing, making it ever more likely that a posse would fetch up there from Cedar Rapids. Kellerman made a decision and called to the men who had surprised him, 'There's only me. There was two of us, but my partner was killed back there. If I come out, will you swear not to gun me down?'

'You've my word,' hollered Ben Walters. Neither Walters nor Jackson could actually see into the cab at that angle and it was quite plausible to suppose that only one man had survived whatever they had been doing. Walters said quietly, 'You stay here and watch. If there's any trickery, then you'll do what's needful.' He shouted again towards the locomotive, 'Throw out your weapon and step down.'

Kellerman said to the 'breed, 'We're running out o' time. You set a watch and start shooting when you've a clear view of who's there. I've a derringer in my boot should all else fail.' Then he tossed his pistol out, where it could be seen by those hiding behind the trees and, raising his hands, moved into view and contrived to clamber down from the cab without lowering his hands; no mean feat. Once his feet were on the ground, Kellerman walked slowly forward, doing his best to compose his features into a semblance of innocence and bewilderment.

Once his man was in sight, Ben Walters stood up and walked out to meet him, his rifle at the ready. When he was a few yards away from the fellow, Walters halted and said, 'I reckon you be Cade Kellerman.'

'That's a fact. Only you is it? By yourself?'

'Not hardly. My boys are keeping us covered. I've a crow to pluck with you. You killed my wife.'

Up until that moment, Ben Walters had not been sure what he was going to do when once he had Kellerman standing before him. Speaking the charge out loud like that had sharpened his mind though. He knew now that he was going to shoot Kellerman down like the mangy cur that he was. Walters raised the rifle to his shoulder, but before he could even take aim there was a crack and the rifle dropped from his nerveless fingers. At the same moment, Kellerman's hand snaked down towards his boot, where he doubtless had some weapon concealed. Three things then happened more or less simultaneously.

As soon as he saw that Walters had been shot, Abernathy Jackson leapt to his feet and drew the heavy pistol with which Walters had insisted he replace the little two-two. He rushed at Kellerman and, seeing that the other man was trying to draw a weapon from his boot, fired at him twice. The first bullet, by sheerest chance, struck Cade Kellerman a mighty blow in the neck. He keeled over, gouts of blood erupting from his throat in pulses. It might have been expected that at this point Jimmy Storm-cloud would gun down the man who had done for his boss, but at that moment the 'breed heard the chugging of an engine and, glancing backwards, he saw that a train was approaching from the rear. He was not so quixotic as to wish to delay his escape for even long enough to revenge his partner. Instead, he hopped down from the opposite side of the cab from where Jackson was standing and went loping off across the open country.

Heedless of all else, least of all of the man he had just shot, Jackson ran over to where Ben Walters was lying. The old man said quietly, 'Well son, you did what you set out to do. You settled with that villain.'

'How bad are you hurt, sir? There doesn't seem to be too much blood.'

'Ah, it's all up with me,' said Walters casually, 'I reckon I'm bound for glory. Or the other place.'

Mortifyingly, Abernathy Jackson found his eyes filling with tears at these words. He said, 'I'll get you to hospital. We can use that locomotive, maybe.'

'No,' said Walters, with absolute finality, 'I'm hit right in the lung. Every breath pains me. Just let me be, boy. I'll be with my wife directly.' He closed his eyes and said faintly, 'Jennifer.'

There was a noise of confused shouting and then a few shots. Jackson looked up in alarm to see five men, advancing menacingly, with drawn pistols. One of them said harshly, 'Throw down your piece or you're as good as dead.'

'It ain't me you're wanting. This here's a sheriff. His name's Ben Walters. That there's Cade Kellerman.' He glanced down at Walters and realized that the old man had stopped breathing.

'Sheriff? We're from Pinkertons. You tellin' me as this fellow took Kellerman down before we got here?' There was a note of disappointment in the man's voice, which disgusted Jackson.

'I sent the telegram to you people. Telling that Kellerman was in Cedar Rapids.'

'The hell you did. Why?'

'I wanted a job. Mr Pinkerton said he'd give me one, if I brought him some intelligence.'

It dawned on the leader of the Pinkertons men that he was in a fair way of being cheated of any glory in this business. This youth had found Kellerman and notified head office and now he'd dealt with him before he and his men even fetched up on the scene. The youngster stood up and began walking away. 'Hey, where you goin'?' asked the Pinkertons man.

'To get my horse. I need to get back to town.'

'You're going for to make out some report on this for the boss?'

'No,' said Abernathy Jackson, sadly, 'If this dirty

business is what it means to be a detective, I reckon as it's not for me. I killed one man and seen another die right in front of me. I guess that's about enough.'

'Seriously though,' called the man after him, 'You don't want credit for this?'

Abernathy turned and stared at the fellow, not bothering to disguise the contempt he fell. He said, 'Credit? You want the credit for this day's work, you take it, mister. Take it and welcome.'

And so it was that Abernathy Jackson discovered, early enough that it didn't wreck his future prospects as a lawyer, that not every man is cut out for a career in law enforcement. It is why to this day the credit for tracking down and disposing of the man behind the Maple Bluff Outrage is given wholly and directly to the Pinkertons' agency and no account of this case ever mentions the name of either Ben Walters or Abernathy Jackson.